MW01148150

LOVE ON FIRE

STARS #2

E. L. TODD

Hartwick Publishing

Love on Fire

Copyright © 2019 by E. L. Todd

All rights reserved.

No part of this book may be reproduced in any form or by any electronic or mechanical means, including information storage and retrieval systems, without written permission from the author, except for the use of brief quotations in a book review.

CONTENTS

1

CHARLOTTE

SUMMER TURNED INTO FALL, AND IT WAS THE LONGEST PERIOD of my life. Time passed so slowly, every day feeling like an eternity. When Neil returned, we would only be friends... but I missed him like crazy anyway. He had become such an integral part of my life, and when he wasn't there, I felt lost.

I sat across the table from Max, a guy I'd met at the gym. We'd flirted back and forth then he asked me to dinner. We went to a taco bar with the best chips and salsa in Texas, but the food couldn't make up for the boring date.

Max wasn't my type.

He was a lot more vocal in the gym, but now he seemed to have forgotten how to speak.

"So, were you born in Texas?"

He finished chewing his chip before he nodded. "Yeah."

This had to be the dullest conversation of my life. "Yeah, me too." Thanks for asking.

He was a handsome guy with a fit body, but everything else about him was boring. If I were just looking for sex, he still wouldn't have fit the bill because there was no chemistry. I wasn't sure if he was just nervous now that we were face-to-face...or maybe he didn't know how to talk to anyone unless he was flirting.

My phone started to ring, and Stacy's name was on the screen. I picked it up, not to be rude, but to explain to her now wasn't the best time. "Hey, Stacy. I'm on a date right now. Can I call you back?"

Max kept eating the chips, watching me with an expressionless face.

"No. I really need to talk to you."

"Uh...is everything okay?" I didn't tell her to pull this stunt, to call when the date was going bad so I could ditch. Maybe she just sensed it? We were best friends, so it was possible... Maybe she could read my mind.

"No. I just found out some terrible news... I thought you'd want to know."

An image of Neil's handsome face popped into my mind. What if something happened at the station at the moon? What if something went wrong? What if he was in trouble? "Is Neil okay?"

"It's not about Neil."

"Oh, thank god." My hand moved across my chest, right over my heart. "Then, what is it?"

"It's actually about Cameron..."

"Okay..." Was he in a car accident? Did something happen?

He wasn't my husband anymore, our divorce papers had been finalized a long time ago, so I wasn't his emergency contact. I wasn't the one legally responsible for his health care needs. If something really happened to him, I didn't know how Stacy would know about it before I did.

"I guess he lost the baby..."

The woman carrying his child was so far along, at least eight months pregnant. They probably already had the baby's room ready. They already picked out names. They were expecting a wonderful addition to their family...but now it wouldn't happen. All the pain I felt when the doctor told me I was barren came rushing back. I understood how painful that was...and no one should have to suffer through it. "Thanks for letting me know."

I PARKED on the sidewalk in front of the house where I used to live. Cameron and I used to sit on the front porch and drink lemonade as we watched the fireflies light up the night sky. The early years of our marriage were magical, when we were newlyweds who believed we would be together forever.

I walked up the sidewalk with the flowers laid across my arm. When my feet hit the wooden porch, I heard the old echo I used to notice every day when Cameron came home from work. Summer was coming to a close and fall was slowly approaching, but I could still feel the Texas heat in the air, the humidity that made you sweat constantly. Whenever people came to visit, they couldn't stand it...but I loved it.

I rang the doorbell.

After nearly a minute, footsteps sounded on the hardwood floor inside. Judging from the gait, it was Cameron. I still remembered the exact sound of his footsteps, where the wood used to creak in the right places.

He opened the door, clearly surprised to see me standing there with an arrangement of flowers. He pushed the screen door open and stepped farther outside, wearing jeans and a t-shirt. His brown hair was messy, like he hadn't showered in a couple of days. His normally tanned skin suddenly looked gray, sickly.

I could see his depression so clearly, see the way this was haunting him. He looked worse than I'd ever seen him, worse than when the doctors told us I couldn't have children. He looked like he'd lost the entire world.

It would be easy for me to be angry, for me to see this as revenge. Maybe karma was at work. But even my greatest enemy didn't deserve this kind of pain. I felt terrible for Cameron and the woman he was with. I was devastated to learn I couldn't have children. I couldn't imagine the pain of being pregnant for nine months and then losing that child. It was wrong...so wrong.

He stared at me with pain in his eyes, as if he didn't know how to interact with me because he was still delirious.

"I wanted you guys to have this..." I held out the large arrangement of flowers. "I'm so sorry..."

He took the flowers without looking at them.

There was nothing I could say to make him feel better, nothing I could say to make this situation seem less severe. Maybe coming here hadn't been a good idea.

Maybe the pain was too raw for him right now. I just wanted him to know that I cared, that I was sorry that this happened. "I'm here if you two need anything..." I didn't even know her first name. All I knew was she was a pretty brunette who had been sleeping with my husband when he was still my husband. Anyone else would have been happy this terrible thing happened to them, but that wasn't me.

He finally glanced at the flowers before he looked at me again. "Thank you..."

"Is she doing okay?" I felt bad for referring to her like that, but I had no idea what her name was.

"Vivian just came home from the hospital. She's resting..."

"Is she going to be okay?"

"Yeah, she'll be fine. Just needs to rest for a week or so."

I didn't ask how it happened, if their baby had been still-born. It didn't matter anyway. Miscarriages were common, unfortunately. "Well, I'm just a phone call away if you need something." I turned away and left him on the doorstep as I headed to my truck. It gave me no pleasure seeing his sadness.

"Char."

I hadn't heard him call me that in a year. I stopped at the bottom of the stairs and turned around.

He set the flowers on the table then followed me down the porch.

I crossed my arms over my chest and looked at him, unsure what he would say. I didn't come here to provoke a conversation. I just wanted him to know that I was there for him, that

I would always be there for him even if he wasn't there for me.

"I don't know what to say..." He slid his hands into his front pockets.

"You don't need to say anything, Cameron. I just came here to give my condolences. Nothing else."

He bowed his head and sighed.

It was never my intention to make him feel guilty, to prove anything. Love was the only thing that drove me to that house. "You should go inside and be with Vivian. Good-night, Cameron." I turned away before he could say anything else. It wasn't my place to linger because that house wasn't my home anymore.

His voice followed me. "Goodnight, Char."

KYLE SAT across from me at the table. We'd decided to get dinner after work, heading to our favorite Thai place. He was in dark jeans and a blue collared shirt, his white jacket remaining in his locker at the hospital. His short blond hair was slightly curly at the ends, and his tanned skin complimented his masculine features well. He was a pretty man, and women were chasing him all the time.

He used his chopsticks to grab a pile of noodles. "After what that asshole did to you, I'm surprised you went over there."

"I've never been one to hold a grudge." I stirred the noodles and didn't take a bite.

"It's not about holding a grudge. This is your ex-husband,

the guy who abandoned you because you couldn't get pregnant."

"If he were in a bad car accident, no one would blink an eye if I were there."

"I would. That guy doesn't deserve any compassion from you."

"Come on, Kyle." I knew he acted like a heartless, tough man, but there was more depth to him than that.

"I'm serious. He slept with that woman before he left you—and he got her pregnant."

"I know..."

"So I don't think he deserved flowers and a condolence. That was karma."

"Kyle, don't say that." The person who was hurt the most was an innocent baby. That definitely wasn't karma. That was a travesty. "I wish it hadn't happened. I wish they'd had a healthy baby and were happy."

Kyle looked at me like I was crazy. "You can't be serious."

"I am serious. I know Cameron was an asshole for what he did, but life is short and he should do whatever makes him happy. If he wants to have a child the natural way, then he should do it. If I'm not what he really wants, I'd rather know while I'm still young."

He shook his head slightly. "That's a very mature thing to say...but I still think you're crazy."

"I've spent almost a year mourning my loss. I'm tired of wasting more time on that man. I just want to move on...and be happy."

He took a few bites of his food, his eyes on me the entire time. "So...does that mean you're ready for a serious relationship?"

"Uh...not really. I just had a terrible date with a guy named Max. The dating world exhausts me. I've finally put myself back together, and I don't want to get shattered again even if I do find someone. I want to be like you, just have fun without worrying about my future."

He let his chopstick lean against the side of his bowl as he looked at me. "I don't have fun because I don't want a wife and kids someday. I have fun because I haven't found the woman I want all of those things with."

"Really?" I asked. "I've never gotten that impression from you."

"Then maybe you don't know me very well."

"You just don't talk about the woman you're seeing very often."

He shrugged. "When there's something to talk about, I'll talk about it."

I grabbed a piece of chicken with my chopsticks and placed it into my mouth.

"Just because Cameron shattered your heart doesn't mean the next guy will. I wouldn't even call that guy a man. There are real men out there, men who will be loyal and committed to their woman until it kills them." He rested his elbows on the table and watched me. "Don't let Cameron ruin a future you haven't even had a chance to experience."

Neil was the first guy I'd met who made me feel comfortable. He was honest and kind, becoming a part of my family without being in my life very long. He was handsome, smart, and built like a brick house. Being something more with him didn't seem so scary, but that was never going to happen. We didn't want the same things...and we were just friends. That meant I had to give someone else a try. "I guess I just need more time. I went on a date with a guy the other night...so damn boring. There was a spark at the gym when we were flirting back and forth, but when we sat down together, it was the most awkward thing in the world. We had nothing to talk about."

"Maybe he just wasn't the right guy."

"He definitely wasn't the right guy..." My mind wandered back to those late nights when Neil and I would get a Slurpee at the gas station. I would drive him home, or he would come over to my place. The sex was great, even better than it had been with Cameron, and that closeness had been there too...that intimacy. But Neil was a man I could never have, so I didn't even bother entertaining the idea. I did miss him, though. He'd been gone for almost three months, and I had no contact with him. I wondered how his work was going, if he was safe. I wondered if he thought about me...or he'd forgotten about me the second his rocket achieved lift-off.

"Then keep looking for the right guy. I know he's out there."

I shrugged. "Yeah...maybe." Even if I could find the right guy, I would never believe in forever. Every relationship had an expiration date; every relationship had its breaking point. Cameron and I were the happiest couple in the world...until tragedy struck. It divided us so deeply.

Kyle continued to watch me with his sky blue eyes. He didn't say a single word, but he didn't need to. He could read my emotions well, understand me the way Stacy did. He understood when I was harboring pain and trying to pretend it wasn't happening. His eyes shifted back and forth slightly, his broad shoulders relaxed. "He's out there, Char. I promise you."

2

CHARLOTTE

"I would have shoved those flowers up his ass." Stacy sat across from me at the dining table in her kitchen.

I swirled my large glass of wine and took a big drink, my eyes slightly lidded because I was already a bit buzzed.

"No, you wouldn't. If this were Vic, you would have done no such thing."

"You bet your ass, I would. If the love of my life did that to me, I would never get over it. Imagining Vic with another woman..." She shook her head. "I would lose my shit. I would turn into a psycho ex that never quits."

I didn't take her response seriously because I was absorbed in that bottle of wine. "Vic would never do that to you, so you have nothing to worry about."

"I would have said the same about Cameron..."

He used to look at me like he was deeply in love with me, that slight softening of his eyes that was so easy to read. I never doubted his love for me, never worried about him going out with his friends because he was so loyal. But all of that changed when the circumstances were different. "Yeah, but Vic is a better man." Maybe I'd been wrong about Cameron. Maybe I was so deeply under the veil of infatuation that I'd viewed the world unrealistically. "And I wasn't always this calm. When things first went down, I was livid. You remember..."

"But that didn't last long. You turned depressed and just stayed there."

And I was still there now.

"And the date didn't go well?"

I shook my head. "He's cute but dull."

"That's too bad. Did you get laid?"

"No. I left to see Cameron afterward. And even if you hadn't called me, I still wouldn't have gone home with him. Not enough chemistry. Not enough anything."

"Being single...it sucks."

I didn't remember it being this hard because I settled down with Cameron. I continued to drink my red wine and not let my thoughts wander to the man stationed on the moon. Sometimes I googled him late at night just to look at his picture—not because I was having a date with my vibrator, but because I just missed those brown eyes and kind smile. I missed my friend. Every time I thought about him, the hole inside my chest got bigger...the void stretching infinitely.

"Have the sellers responded to your offer yet?"

There was a house I was interested in just outside Houston. It was a three-bedroom house with a reasonable backyard for Torpedo. It also had the wraparound porch that I told my real estate agent was a requirement. "No. But I didn't go far under the asking price. It should work out. And if they do accept my offer, I can move in immediately."

"I hope so. Such a beautiful place."

After I'd heard about Cameron's tragedy, I lost all my excitement for the new place. All I could think about was his pain. I knew exactly how he felt, to want a family you couldn't have. "I'll miss living at Neil's."

"Because of that backyard?"

I shrugged. "I just like the atmosphere. Even when he's not there, I can feel him. I can still smell his cologne on the couches, feel his presence when I see his medals on the wall. It's comforting."

With her fingers wrapped around her glass, she watched me with shrewd eyes. "You miss him, don't you?"

I could shrug off her question with a lie, but I didn't feel like pretending. "Yes."

"He'll be home in a week. You think you guys will pick up where you left off?"

A part of me wished we could be lovers again, tangled up in the sheets together, using each other's bodies to feel good. He was the best sex I'd ever had, and even if it was ultimately meaningless, it meant the world to me. But he was too important to throw away, to get caught up in a bitter falling-out that made both of us uncomfortable. There was no future with him, just heartbreak. It was best to be friends so he would always be part of my life. I'd probably always have feelings for him, feel a thrill down my spine when he entered the room, but that was better than losing him altogether. "No. We agreed to be friends...and that's what will happen."

Stacy gave me an incredulous look, her eyebrow raised in disbelief. "You really believe that?"

"Yes. That's the only option we have. There's no future together, and if things get messy, it'll make everything complicated. That's the last thing either one of us wants. He wants to be a bachelor forever. I want to have a family someday."

"So, you do want to get remarried? Because for the last nine months you've said otherwise."

I shrugged. "I guess I'm more open to the idea now, but I'm skeptical. The only thing that gives me hope that it's still possible is Vic. I see the way he loves you, and I believe someone will love me that way."

"Yes, that's very possible," she said firmly. She refilled her glass of water and took another drink. "Have you ever considered going out with Kyle?"

It wasn't the first time she'd mentioned him. "No."

"He's pretty hot."

"He's my friend."

"You can't put every guy you like in the friend zone. Otherwise, you'll have no men to screw."

"Kyle and I have been friends for a long time, and I want it to stay that way." He was my rock, the person I could say anything to without judgment. We liked the same things, like hiking and bowling. I'd helped him pick up women a few times, pretending to be a heartbroken woman who got rejected by him.

"You've slept with him before."

"Because I was depressed out of my mind. I wasn't thinking clearly."

"But you said he was good in bed."

"Yeah, but that doesn't change anything."

She gripped her glass between her fingertips. "Are you still attracted to him?"

Stacy was pushing Kyle on me, and Kyle had made a comment about us in the past. I didn't take him seriously at the time, but now it seemed like something was going on right under my nose. "Yes, I think Kyle is hot. But I'm not interested in a romantic relationship with him. He's my friend, and I wouldn't jeopardize that for anything. He means too much to me."

"Cameron really messed you up. Now you're making all the good men off-limits because you're afraid to lose them. That leaves the shitty men you don't care about losing. You're making your pool of potential guys very small."

"Neil is different. He's made it clear he doesn't want anything serious. Ever."

"If he felt otherwise, would things be different?"

"I don't know," I said with a shrug. "I'm still in a dark place, so I'm not sure."

Vic walked in the door with a device under his arm. Thankfully, he had stepped inside and interrupted our conversation because I didn't want to talk about it anymore. "I've got good news."

"You're taking me to dinner and then sexing me up?" Stacy

asked without turning to look at him.

With a slight grin, he joined us at the dining table. "You're right about the second part, but not the first."

"You can't take your woman out for a nice meal?" she asked, still gripping her wine.

He sat at the head of the table. "Why? You'll put out anyway."

She glared at him maliciously with her eyes, but the slight smile on her lips gave her true feelings away.

"What's your good news?" I asked.

He turned the device around so we could see the screen. "NASA sent me a message from Neil."

I hadn't seen his face or heard his voice in a long time, unless I looked up old YouTube videos. I watched an episode of him as the guest on a nightly talk show, and I even saw a clip of him meeting the president. The guy was America's hero, a man so charming and handsome he was loved by everyone. "Great. What did he say?"

"Haven't watched it yet." He set it down then opened the video and hit play.

Neil was in front of the screen, wearing a black t-shirt while he sat at a desk. Behind him was a gray wall, and the desk in front of him showed a couple of tools I didn't recognize. His brown hair was slightly messy like he'd just woken up, and his skin was paler than it usually was, probably because he didn't get much sun exposure while on the moon. But there was no doubt he was just as sexy as he'd always been. "Hey, Vic. Hope things are well at home. You said your wife should be knocked up by the time I return. That better be true." He smiled slightly, his brown eyes lighting up in his charismatic way. He had such handsome features, a strong jaw and noticeable cheekbones. And his eyes relayed his kindness, the windows to his soul. "I sent Mom a video too, but I have a feeling she may not watch it. If that's the case, give her my best and tell her I'll return to Earth in a week. We're getting ready for the launch as we speak."

I stared at his image on the screen and sighed quietly. "Man...he's so hot."

Vic and Stacy both turned to me, their eyebrows raised.

"What?" I asked innocently. "He is. He's the most beautiful man I've ever seen."

Stacy chuckled. "Yeah...I'm sure you'll just be friends when he gets back."

"We will," I said firmly. "But I can't think he's sexy?"

Vic turned back to the screen, keeping his silence on the matter.

Neil kept talking. "NASA sent me here to repair the Rover system. There was some kind of issue with the software so I had to reprogram the entire thing. Took me several weeks to accomplish it, and then I've worked on a few other projects while I've been stationed here." Sometimes his eyes drifted away from the screen, just the way it would during a normal conversation. "But I'm leaving in a week. We'll return to Earth in the shuttle. I'm excited to see you guys."

I didn't expect Neil to mention me at all. I was just a friend, and this message wasn't meant to be seen by me. But it was nice to hear his voice, to see his gorgeous brown eyes and his strong shoulders. It'd been three months since I'd gotten laid. Just looking at him got me hot everywhere.

There was a long pause, like Neil was carefully considering what to say next. His arms weren't as sculpted as they had been before he left, but the veins were still noticeable. His hand moved to his chin, and he rubbed his fingers across his freshly shaved skin. "Give Charlotte my best. I hope she's doing well."

Butterflies soared in my stomach, and my heart fluttered the second I heard my name from his lips. Knowing I was on his mind and in his heart made me feel special. There were so many people he knew on Earth, and I was one of the few he was thinking about.

"I expect there will be a bunch of dog hair on my couch when I get back." He smiled like that didn't bother him in the least. "I look forward to seeing it." He turned his head to the right, as if he was looking at someone offscreen. Then he turned back to us. "I'll see you soon. Love you guys." He reached for the mouse beside him and clicked the button to end the video.

Vic shut the device and looked at his wife. "It's been a long three months..."

"He'll definitely be home for a long time," Stacy said. "He's done two trips back-to-back. They won't be sending him up again for awhile. He'll probably be home for years."

"Hope you're right," Vic said.

I was excited Neil was coming home. I couldn't wait to feel those strong arms wrap around me, embrace me with strength. I couldn't wait to see that handsome smile, listen to that deep laugh. A smile formed on my lips now that the wait was almost over. "I'm so happy he's coming home."

3

NEIL

I LAY IN MY COT WITH MY ARM TUCKED UNDER MY HEAD. SINCE the surface of the moon where our station was located constantly faced the Earth, I could always see it outside my window whenever the sun was in the right place.

I'd been staring at the planet every single day for three months. It never looked as beautiful as it did hundreds of thousands of miles away. I could see the world turn and watch the clouds shift as the atmosphere protected it from the harsh radiation from the sun. Earth was so vulnerable but so resilient at the same time. When I was on a barren surface full of rocks and sand that lacked an atmosphere, I came to appreciate our home even more. It was one of a kind, the perfect condition for complex life.

I missed it.

Evelyn walked up to my cot, dressed in cargo pants and a t-shirt. "Can't sleep?"

I turned back to her, my ankles crossed at the edge of the cot. "Just anxious."

She sat on her cot across from me, her hair in a braid over one shoulder. "I thought Commander Neil Crimson would never want to return to Earth."

I loved being deep in space, and the only thing I missed about Earth was gravity. But now I missed summer in the South, missed getting a Slurpee at the local gas station, looking out my back window and seeing a black Lab enjoying the shady spot in the grass. I missed the soft strands of hair that lay across my chest while I slept. There was a small pain in my heart, a discomfort I couldn't describe. "I guess I'm a little homesick. What about you?"

She shrugged. "A bit. I miss my friends and family, but I know when I return to Earth, it'll be years before I can get back up here. So, I'm trying to cherish every moment I can. I'm not the best test pilot in the air force, not the astronaut who's been in space the longest. You'll launch at least a dozen more times in your career. For me...this could be the last time. Not as much need for an astrophysicist up here."

I could say empty words to make her feel better, but that felt like too much work. Pilots launched into space more often because they could dock with the ISS, and they could land the space shuttle on the landing strip in Houston. Scientists had to rely on open seats in order to get to the Lunar Labs or the ISS because they didn't have the skills to fly. I was also an engineer, which enabled me to handle the computer systems if something went wrong. "Maybe this is the last time. But maybe it's not."

"It's always been my dream since I was a young girl. And it's everything I imagined it would be..."

"Then don't be sad that it's over. Be happy that it happened."

She leaned against the wall and pulled her knees to her chest. "What's your favorite part about it?"

I turned my head back to the window and looked at Earth. "This."

"It is incredible, isn't it?" Her voice lowered, and then silence overtook us both.

Together, we stared at Earth...the only place in the galaxy that everyone who's ever lived has called home.

I CLOSED the hatch and began my walk on the surface of the moon. I could hear my own breathing inside the space helmet, and the light on my suit illuminated the terrain underneath my boots. Houston was in my ear.

"All readings clear," the director spoke over the intercom.

Gravity was one-sixth what it was on Earth, so I practically bounced as I walked across the surface. Without the force pulling me to the surface of the planet, it would be assumed that I could get where I needed to go faster, but that wasn't the case. It took me longer because I moved vertically rather than horizontally most of the time. The Aitken Basin was just over the ridge, the largest and oldest crater on the moon. Sixteen hundred miles across and nearly four miles deep, it was beautiful and eerie at the same time. I stopped at the edge and looked down, seeing an infinite shadow stretch all the way to the bottom.

Even with Houston in my ear, spacewalks on the moon were profoundly lonely. Surrounded by darkness and the unknown of space, it was so quiet. If my helmet wasn't on, I couldn't even hear my own breathing. Without air or an atmosphere, I couldn't make a sound at all. I couldn't scream for help.

It was the most humbling experience.

People were surprised by my lack of arrogance on Earth. I was a famous man with a famous face. People described me as brilliant. Others considered me courageous. And many others considered me the most desirable bachelor on the planet. But once your feet had left the surface of our planet, it was abundantly clear how insignificant you were.

I was nothing.

The universe was millions of years old, and there were billions and billions of stars in the sea of nothingness. It made our planet insignificant. And if eight billion people were insignificant, what did that make me?

Insignificant.

I kneeled down and scooped up a handful of sand before placing it inside a secured plastic bag. I sealed the top and placed it into my pocket.

Houston spoke over the intercom. "What's your status, Neil? Do you see something?"

I continued to walk forward and disregarded their inquiry. They probably realized my position on the satellite had turned ideal. "About to step down into the crater, Houston. Everything is good on my end."

LUNAR LABS COULD ACCOMMODATE six astronauts, just as at the ISS. There were only three of us now because the previous three astronauts stationed there had returned to

Earth. We stayed behind because each of us still had work to do.

Now it was a bit lonely.

There was a sense of camaraderie between us, but we each had very different disciplines. Evelyn was the first astrophysicist in space, and she worked with the satellites we had positioned on the dark side of the moon. Simon was a biologist, and he was a smart guy, just withdrawn and quiet.

There was some chemistry between Evelyn and me, but that was a line I would never cross.

NASA didn't have any rules in regards to personal relationships between astronauts, but I thought that was the dumbest idea in the world. Even though I was alone on the moon, I still wouldn't give in to temptation because it was completely unprofessional. I wasn't really interested anyway...just lonely.

To my surprise, I thought about Charlotte more than I expected. I'd imagined I would think about her for the first few weeks I was away, and then she would fade from my mind. In actuality, my longing for her increased as weeks turned into months. Now that the mission was over, I was most excited to see her.

I missed her.

Our physical relationship was over, and now, we would just be friends.

But just a friendship with her was so fulfilling. It cured my loneliness, made me feel complete in a way my other lovers never did. I couldn't wait to see her smile again, see the blue Slurpee stain her teeth and make her cute. I couldn't wait to hear that laugh, see her sexy legs in those cutoff jeans.

But then a terrible idea hit me.

She could be with a guy.

It'd been three months...she could be serious with another guy.

She could even be with Kyle.

She was just my friend, so it shouldn't matter who she was with, even if it was Kyle. But it still turned me inside out and made me sick...which was impressive because I could withstand an incredible amount of g-force without getting nauseated. But just the thought of Kyle finally getting what he wanted made me never want to return to Earth so I wouldn't have to watch it.

4

CHARLOTTE

Kyle and Vic helped me move in to my new place.

"Right here is good." I pointed to the spot on the rug.

The guys carried the heavy piece of furniture inside and set it down, their strong muscles flexing.

Torpedo sat in the corner, his eyes following the guys in their movements.

Stacy came in next with the throw pillows for the couch. "It's not even done, and it already looks great."

It was a great milestone in life, purchasing my first home. I did it all by myself, my private jab at Cameron. He left me destitute and kept the house, but I landed back on my feet all on my own. "Thanks. Torpedo likes it too."

Kyle walked into the kitchen and grabbed a water. Sweat poured down his forehead and arms, and he looked like a workout model in a TV commercial. The more Stacy pointed him out, the more I noticed all his charms. I understood why women were always interested in him, not just because he was handsome, but because he was thoughtful and kind.

"Need help with anything else?" Stacy asked. "I could pick up something heavier than a few pillows."

"Forget it." Vic moved his hand over her stomach, sprinkling her with a subtle touch of affection. "You aren't moving a damn thing." He walked back outside and headed to the moving truck parked on the street.

I stared at Stacy, my eyebrow arched so high. "Girl..."

She could barely hide her smile. Her cheeks reddened and she looked at the ground, hiding her embarrassment as best she could. Then her hand slid gently across her stomach, and the glow of her skin suddenly became obvious.

"Oh. My. God."

She finally released a sigh and squealed. "Yes, I'm pregnant."

"That's amazing." I moved into her arms and hugged her tightly, feeling happy for my best friend. She and Vic had been looking forward to this for years, and now the moment had finally arrived. "I'm so happy for you."

"I wasn't sure how to tell you. With everything that happened—"

"You have nothing to worry about." I pulled away so she could see my expression. "I'm very happy for you. I'm going to be an aunt. It's such an honor." I'd wanted to have my own children, and sometimes I wondered how different my life would have been if Cameron and I could have gotten pregnant. I always pictured myself running around with two kids. It was hard watching someone experience the beauty of motherhood, but I was genuinely happy for her. "You and

Vic are going to be awesome parents. And when this baby starts to drive you crazy, I can babysit with Torpedo."

"Can I get that in writing?" she teased.

Vic walked back inside, and when he saw us together, he figured out what just happened. "Figured out I knocked up my wife?"

"Yep. Congratulations." I hugged him next.

"Thanks." He squeezed me hard then patted me on the back. "Now we just need to find a house before this baby gets here."

"I'm sure you'll find something that has everything you're looking for."

Kyle came next and hugged them both. "Congratulations. That's really exciting."

"We're so happy." Stacy rubbed her stomach. "I'm only a few weeks along, so we shouldn't be telling people, but we can't keep it from you two."

"Neil will be thrilled." I'd been counting down the days until his return, so excited to see him I could barely contain it. He was about to find out he would be an uncle—and that would certainly put a smile on his face.

"Absolutely," Vic said. "I'm the only one who will continue the family line, so he'll definitely be excited about it."

The statement reminded me what Neil's priorities were. He'd given his life to research and exploration, not to romance or marriage. He would never be a husband or a father. And to me, he would only ever be a friend.

I just had to keep that in mind.

THE THREE OF us sat on the couch in the living room, facing the TV as they broadcasted the landing of the shuttle.

Last time I'd watched Neil come back to Earth, there wasn't such trepidation in my veins because he was a stranger to me. Unlike Vic, I was relaxed. I watched the moment objectively, as a stranger witnessing an extraordinary moment. But now, all of that was different because I cared about this man.

I looked worse than Vic.

My body was rigid and tight, my chest constricted. I watched the shuttle enter the atmosphere and approach the landing strip. It wasn't any different from a regular plane landing, but since this one was coming at such an astronomical speed, it felt completely different.

Vic was pale as a ghost.

Stacy rubbed his back as she turned to me. "The shuttles don't have engines."

The only reason I pulled my eyes off the screen was because I was perplexed by what she said. "Don't have engines?"

"They're gliders."

My eyebrows nearly rose off my face. "You're telling me that Neil is landing this plane without an engine?"

She nodded. "So, he has only one chance to get it right."

"Jesus..." Landing from space was already difficult, but doing it with only one try...that was the most terrifying thing I'd ever heard. "Are we certain Neil is flying?"

"Yes," Vic said while keeping his eyes on the TV. "He's the only pilot on the mission."

That made me feel a little better because if anyone could do this, it was him. "Then everything will be fine. He's the best pilot in the world. He'll be okay."

Vic relaxed a little at my words.

The shuttle came closer to the surface, lined up, and then touched the ground perfectly. The parachute deployed from the rear and the shuttle immediately reduced in speed.

Vic released the breath he was holding. "That looked like an easy landing."

"Yeah, it did." I stared at the screen and watched the shuttle come to a slow stop. NASA officially came out to retrieve them from the craft. Mesmerized, I watched Neil exit the shuttle and step onto the asphalt, wearing his space suit with his helmet held in his hand. Looking regal, handsome, and like a damn superhero when he smiled brighter than the sun. "But Neil makes everything look easy."

5

CHARLOTTE

NEIL STAYED OVERNIGHT AT THE SPACE CENTER SO HE COULD be examined for foreign bacteria or other pathogens that could do harm to the American people. He'd been to the moon many times and it had been concluded that the moon was simply a barren rock, but NASA kept the protocol anyway.

The next morning, I went to his house with Vic and Stacy.

"Miss it?" Stacy asked as she sat on the living room couch.

I shrugged. "A bit. Staying here made me despise my apartment. I realized Torpedo and I need to live in a house. He needs a yard. But I also felt honored to stay in his house, to live in a world-famous astronaut's home."

Vic rolled his eyes. "I see him as my obnoxious older brother, not some superhero."

Stacy elbowed him in the stomach. "Shut up. Yes, you do."

Vic shrugged it off.

I was excited to see Neil walk through the door, but I was also nervous. It'd been three months since I last saw his face, from the moment he kissed me goodbye in front of his family. It was the best kiss I'd ever had, an epic embrace before he walked off, looking majestic in his glowing white suit. It was a scene from a movie, the most romantic moment of my life.

Even though Neil Crimson didn't do romance.

The jitters ran through my veins, and my stomach was tight with anticipation. Just seeing his face on the screen a week ago brought me so much joy. The man I missed would walk through that door any minute, no doubt wearing that panty-melting smile.

But I had to remember he was just my friend...and nothing more.

We heard a car door closing, all of us slightly jumping at the sound. Then we all looked at one another.

"That's probably him," I whispered.

"Yeah," Stacy said in agreement.

Vic moved to the front door and opened it.

Neil was halfway up the path, carrying his black leather bag in his grasp. He was in jeans and his signature blue NASA jacket, looking exactly the way he had when he'd returned from space months ago. His eyes lit up when he looked at his younger brother, his gaze filled with deep affection.

He set his bag down and embraced his brother. His arms wrapped around Vic's body, and his palm cupped the back of his head. They squeezed each other before Neil clapped him hard on the back. "So, did you knock up your wife like you promised?"

Vic pulled away, smiled, and then gave a nod. "You know I'm a man of my word."

Neil's face lit up in a whole new way. "Awesome." He clapped him on the arm again. "Another little Crimson running around."

"Just don't fill his head with ideas of space and fighter jets."

"That's gonna be pretty hard since that's my job."

"Well, just don't talk about it."

"Your kid is gonna think I'm way cooler than you. Get over it."

Vic chuckled and rolled his eyes at the same time. "Asshole..." He picked up Neil's bag and moved out of the way so Neil could enter the house.

He embraced Stacy next. "Congratulations." He hugged her hard and pulled her into his chest, not giving her those gentle embraces between two strangers. This was a real hug, an even deeper one than he gave his own brother.

"Thank you, Neil."

"For everyone's sake, I hope this kid gets your looks and brains."

She chuckled. "My husband is a very sexy man. I'd love to have a son who looks just like him."

"If you say so." He released her then turned his gaze on me. He gave me a different look than he gave his family. His eyes were still soft and his shoulders strong, but a quiet sigh escaped his lips, like seeing me was more emotional than seeing the other two. He stopped in front of me, as if he was remembering that he couldn't lift me off my feet and kiss me the way he used to. Now we were just two friends...two platonic people who would never mean anything to each other.

Now that I could see how handsome he was, I wished that weren't the case. He'd slimmed down a bit, probably because he'd been on a space diet of dehydrated food for three months. He didn't have any weight to lose to begin with, so his muscle tone had decreased. But he definitely was just as sexy as he'd always been.

I wanted to say something to break the ice, but words weren't forthcoming. I was frozen to my core, caught off guard even though I'd known he was coming. I couldn't force a smile to seem happy. I couldn't do anything besides feel the emotion overwhelm me. "I'm so glad you're okay."

A slight smile moved into his lips. "I'll always be okay, Slurpee." His arms moved around my waist, and he pulled me into his chest. His large arms tightened around my body and cradled me close, his fingers grabbing the fabric of my t-shirt and gently pulling on it. His chin rested on my head, and he held me for so long, it didn't seem like he would let me go.

I never wanted him to let me go.

He probably didn't wear cologne on his mission, so what I smelled now was just him...the scent of masculine soap. My arms rested on his, and I let my check press against the cotton of his shirt, press against the hardness of his chest. I closed my eyes and felt so relaxed, like I could drift off to sleep and never wake up again. Being in this man's arms was like being home.

When he pulled away, I almost didn't let him go.

"How did you like my place?" He stepped back, taking his comforting touch with him.

I almost forgot to respond because I was still reeling from his distance. "It was comfortable. Torpedo and I had a good time."

"Are you guys still here?" He looked over my shoulder and to the back yard, as if he expected Torpedo to be resting under his favorite tree.

"No. I bought a house."

His mouth stretched into a smile, but his eyes contained his disappointment. "Wow...that's great. Congratulations. Where is it?"

"A few miles from here, closer to the city."

"How does Torpedo like it?"

"It's a downgrade compared to here, but he's happy."

"Did you bring him with you?"

"No," I said as I shook my head. "I was afraid he would knock you down and slobber all over you."

"I wouldn't have minded. But I guess I can always see him later."

Vic came farther into the house and placed the black duffel bag on the couch. "So, how do you feel?"

Now that our private conversation was over, Neil turned to his brother. "A little disoriented. It always takes a while to get used to gravity."

"Are they letting you take a vacation?" Vic moved to one of the couches and took a seat.

Neil chuckled, sitting in the lone recliner. "They just sent me to the moon. To them, that's a vacation."

"Even if they let you take a vacation, you would never take it." Stacy moved to the spot beside Vic, and instantly, they turned affectionate. Her hand moved to his thigh, and she scooted close to him, more in love than ever before because of the baby growing inside her.

I moved to the other couch—alone.

Neil nodded. "You're probably right. I have a lot of stuff to do in Houston anyway."

While others considered him a workaholic, I admired his dedication. He believed in his work so much, he was willing to sacrifice everything for it. He faced the steepest odds because of his advancements for humankind.

"Enough about me." Neil leaned forward with his elbows resting on his knees. "When is the kid gonna be here?"

"She's only a month along, so we have a long way to go." Vic rested his hand on hers. "But we're very excited, and we intend to get a house before they arrive. Need to set up the nursery, get a bunch of supplies, etc."

"Does Mom know?" Neil asked.

Vic shook his head. "We wanted to wait until you got back."

Neil looked away as if he was touched. "Thanks..."

It was hard for me to deny my attraction, the growing infatuation I had for this man. I had to constantly remind myself he was just my friend now. I needed to see him as such, to ignore his muscular arms and his pretty eyes. Maybe if I had a man in my life, I wouldn't be so hard up, but I didn't want to pursue someone just to forget about the man I actually wanted. I'd done that with Kyle, and that was a big mistake. Thankfully, it didn't ruin our friendship.

"Anything else new with you guys?" Neil acted like our lives were just as interesting as his, even though that wasn't possible.

"You're the one who went to the moon," Vic said. "Tell us about it."

"Well..." Neil's gaze focused on a random spot on the wall as he reflected on the past few months. "It took a few weeks to repair the Rover software. All the vehicles were on hiatus, which was halting various research programs. It put a lot of astronauts behind, but hopefully they can make up for lost time."

"What did you do for the rest of the time?" Vic asked. "Since that only took a couple of weeks?"

"Picked up other projects NASA wanted me to take care of," Neil answered. "There's always work to do, never any downtime."

"Who were you with?" Stacy asked.

"Mostly two other astronauts," Neil explained. "One is an astrophysicist, so she was working with the satellites most of the time. Another was a biologist. He's conducting experiments with flora in newly constructed greenhouses."

"Wow, how's that going?" Vic asked.

Neil shrugged. "They grow at a different rate because of the gravity, but it's clear there's no possibility of life on the moon, even through artificial means. But it's nice to know we can grow crops."

"What's the difference in gravity of the moon compared to Earth?" It was an honor to have someone so knowledgeable right in the living room. He had so much information in that beautiful head of his, had so much experience we couldn't conceive of. But he remained humble—always.

His answer came out instantly. "The moon possesses about one-sixth of Earth's gravity."

"Wow..." I couldn't even comprehend that. It had significantly less gravity, but people on the moon didn't drift away. "What's the difference between us and Mars?"

When Neil looked at me, his eyes narrowed slightly, as if the question provoked him. "Why do you ask that?" It was an odd question to ask, especially since he seemed a little flustered by it.

"Um...they always say that one day we'll go to Mars. I was just curious." I didn't see the harm in the question. He was always thrilled when I asked him questions about space, but this time, he almost seemed offended by it.

Neil was quiet for a while before he answered. "It's one-third of Earth's gravity."

"Oh," Stacy said. "So, there's no point in exploring Mars as a suitable planet. If the gravity is only one-third, we could never live there."

"I wouldn't say that," Neil replied, not making eye contact with anyone.

"Is it strong enough to hold oxygen and the atmosphere to the surface?" I asked.

"Barely," Neil answered. "There's strong evidence that Mars did have an atmosphere at one point in time, with oceans and streams. It's not impossible that all of that could be reversed under the right conditions."

I raised an eyebrow, repeating what he said in my head. "Are you saying it really is possible for humans to live on Mars?"

He stared at the ground for a moment then shrugged. "It's not impossible...that's all I know." He rose to his feet and headed to the kitchen. "Anyone want a drink? I'm sure I've got some beer around here somewhere..."

6

NEIL

"So, what went haywire?" Hyde sat across from me at the table in the bar, drinking a dark IPA, his chin covered with a beard. He brought the glass to his lips once in a while for a drink, and he always licked his lips afterward. "Systems like that don't just stop working. Getting a virus is nearly impossible, and I doubt one of the engineers screwed something up."

I'd been home for nearly two weeks. Acclimating to gravity was always hard, but it was especially difficult this time around because I'd had such a short break between my two missions. My intestines were used to floating, and they protested the pull of gravity the second they were exposed to it. I was slightly nauseated for the first week because my pH was out of whack. It got easier with every passing day, and the physicians at the Space Center assured me I was perfectly healthy. It would just take time to unwind. "I have no idea. It was something in the system on the moon. I had to wipe the software and reprogram it."

"But you don't know what was wrong?"

I shook my head. "No idea. All I knew was, I had to start from scratch."

"That's so odd. I've never seen that before."

"Neither have I."

"At least that got you another trip to the moon."

As much as I loved every launch, I would have appreciated more time on Earth. I had bigger fish to fry. "I suppose. When do you launch?"

"Two months from now. NASA hasn't told me what my mission is yet."

"You have no idea where you're going?" There were only two options, but they made a difference.

"The moon, which is exciting because they usually send me to ISS."

"Yes, that is exciting."

He took a drink of his beer. "Is your cute little friend excited that you're home?"

There was only one woman he could be referring to, but I played dumb. "You tell me."

His eyes narrowed as he glared. "You better not be calling me your cute little friend."

"What?" I asked innocently. "You're definitely cute."

He rolled his eyes. "Have you seen her yet?"

"The day I got back."

"And?"

"And what?" I asked. "We're just friends now."

"Why?" Hyde cocked his head. "She's hot."

"Whoa...what would Jane think of that?"

"Oh, come on," he snapped. "She knows she's the only woman for me. She also knows I'm not oblivious to everything around me. So, what the hell, Neil? You seemed to like her."

"We agreed to just be friends."

"Why would you agree to something like that?" He leaned back in his chair and crossed his arms over his chest. "You obviously like her."

She deserved a good husband and a man who would be a great father. I couldn't offer her the fairy tale she wanted. Even if she didn't want those things, I was a man who would never be around. "I'm not looking for a relationship."

"Who said anything about a relationship?"

"She wants something serious, so she shouldn't waste her time with me." I wondered if Kyle had made his move yet. It'd been three months, so she was probably ready to move on with her life. The guy was biding his time in the shadows, waiting for the perfect time to get the woman he wanted. I'd be lying if I said it didn't make me jealous.

"That's lame." He drank his beer again.

There were several times I'd considered calling her, asking her to get a drink and catch up. I always changed my mind because I was afraid where that request might lead. She could probably control herself around me, but could I do the same?

"If you aren't going to budge, does that mean there's already a new woman on your radar?"

By now, there usually would be someone else in my bed. Women were easy to come by, especially when most of them recognized me from my appearances on late-night shows and wherever else my face was plastered. Despite my dry spell, I wasn't in a rush to get laid. Jerking off was good enough, a luxury I didn't have at the Lunar Labs because privacy was nearly impossible to come by. "Not really. But give it time."

"So, ARE YOU MORE EXCITED?" I asked. "Or more scared?"

Vic sat on the other couch, holding a beer close to his mouth without taking a drink. "Both."

"Hyde told me he was scared shitless to be a father. When we'd work together, he would find anything to do just so he didn't have to go home. Every time he looked at Jane, he was reminded that the baby was coming...and he'd lose his resolve."

"I'm not that bad. Stacy's little belly is sexy. When I look at her, I just want to fuck her."

I chuckled despite the crass comment. "Romantic..."

"You'll see what I mean someday."

No, I really wouldn't. "Found a house yet?" We were in their apartment, the two of us in the living room in front of the TV. Stacy must still be at work because she hadn't come home and started dinner.

"No, but we've been looking. I want to be close to work, but Stacy wants a huge yard, lots of privacy, the whole nine yards."

"Doesn't she want to be close to work too?"

He set his beer on the table. "No. She'll be a stay-at-home mom now."

"Really?" I asked. "She's okay with that?"

"That's what she wants. She said she only worked so she had something to do, and now that she has something to focus on, she prefers that over working."

"And how do you feel about that?" My brother had become a successful litigator right after college. He made good money overnight, making him a desirable bachelor to every single woman. But Stacy never seemed to care about his money.

"I think it's great. I hate the idea of a babysitter or day care."

"True."

Footsteps sounded in the hallway, along with a pair of loud voices. "Can you believe that?" Char's voice was easily recognizable. "Never, ever, in my whole life, has that ever happened to me."

"It's kinda sexy, if you ask me," Stacy responded. "They were both decent-looking." She opened the door and stepped inside first, carrying a to-go container of food. She set the plastic bag on the counter.

My eyes immediately went to Charlotte, who was wearing denim jeans with holes in the material and a black t-shirt that hugged the swell of her perfect rack. Her hair was straight and shiny. Her figure was just as sexy as I remembered, and those eyes still made my stomach tumble with somersaults.

"About time you brought some food." Vic walked into the

living room and pulled the containers from the plastic bag. "What'd you get?"

Stacy put one hand on her hip, glaring at my brother. "Uh, hello?"

"Hi." Vic didn't even look at her as he grabbed the food along with two paper plates.

"Wow, your pregnant wife brings you food, and I barely get some eye contact?" Stacy asked, her attitude in full force.

Vic abandoned the food and turned to her. In one fluid motion, he backed her into the fridge as he slid his hand into her hair and kissed her like no one was watching. His body pressed against hers, and they become locked together in a heated embrace, a sexy moment that was beyond PG-13.

Charlotte watched them with red cheeks then looked away, her eyes finally settling on me.

I shrugged and gave a slight smile.

She smiled back—cute as ever. "Anyway..." She walked into the living room and sat on my couch but chose the cushion on the opposite side. "I was gonna get a beer, but I guess I'll wait."

"It looks like you're gonna wait a long time."

She chuckled. "If she weren't already pregnant, I'd say she's about to get pregnant..."

Vic finally broke apart from Stacy, grabbed the food, and walked off like nothing happened.

Stacy continued to lean against the fridge, her fingertips covering her lips while her eyes looked distant. Like she was a schoolgirl, a smile spread across her lips.

Vic slid the container toward me across the table then opened his. Inside was a roast beef sandwich with cheddar cheese along with fries. Mine was the same. He picked it up with both hands and took a large bite as if he hadn't just had a make-out session with his wife against the fridge.

"What happened to you that you thought would never, ever happen?" I leaned forward with my elbows on my knees and looked at her. I was hungry, craving the fat sandwich right in front of me after eating space food for so long, but her pretty face was far more entertaining.

"Oh." Charlotte rolled her eyes. "Stacy and I got a drink after work, and these two guys came up to me. Basically asked me to have a threesome."

"What?" I blurted, surprised that two guys would be interested in something like that.

She shrugged. "I'm guessing one of them is bisexual. I was super flattered, but not interested."

"And I thought it was hilarious." Stacy had finally recovered from her fluster and opened the fridge to grab some beers. She picked up two then carried one to Charlotte. "It was very flattering. It's not often you get propositioned for crazy sex like that."

It happened to me all the time.

"Maybe I should have said yes," Charlotte said as a joke. "Just so I could say it happened. They were cute..."

Picturing her with another guy, let alone two, immediately made every muscle in my body tighten. But since she'd said no, it also made me laugh. "I'm sure there will be other opportunities."

"I don't know...threesomes aren't common for me."

Vic picked up his sandwich and took enormous bites, focusing on his food and the TV and ignoring our conversation. He must have been starving because he would have been more involved in this conversation otherwise.

"What do you do when you're asked to have a threesome?" Char asked.

I was surprised by the question, and I was even more surprised that I didn't want to answer it. Every man wanted to brag about his sexual conquests, but in this case, I almost felt embarrassed by them. I shrugged in response. "Did you guys get something to eat?"

Her eyes narrowed slightly when I ignored the question, but she didn't press me on it. "Yeah, we both had salads."

Vic kept eating. "Sounds terrible."

Stacy took the seat beside him, cuddling into his side like she wished she were the sandwich he was eating. "I can't gain fifty pounds being pregnant, so I've got to watch my figure."

"Isn't that the best part about being pregnant?" Charlotte asked. "You can grow to any size and still look beautiful."

"But once the baby is here, I'll just look like a fat chick," Stacy responded.

"Skinny or fat, I'll fuck you anyway." Vic kept eating, picking up a few fries and putting them in his mouth.

Stacy rolled her eyes. "Wow, that's sweet..."

"Yes, I'm a very romantic guy," Vic said as he grabbed a handful of fries and placed them in his mouth.

The moment felt comfortable, the four of us hanging out together. It was much better than the perpetual loneliness I'd felt on the moon. But it also felt particularly nice to be with Charlotte. Our chemistry was exactly what it used to be, and as if no time had passed, we got along great. She was easy to talk to, making the conversation effortless.

I missed her.

My eyes kept moving to her face, and I had to force myself to look at my brother or the TV so it wasn't so obvious. I'd been with a lot of beautiful women, some fitter and sexier, but there was something about Charlotte that outshone the rest. It was like I could see her sweet soul right through her skin, see her kindness as if it were a physical feature. I found her compassion, her goodness, far sexier than any pair of legs I'd set eyes on.

But nothing could happen, so I had to knock that shit off.

"Has the adjustment to Earth been easy?" she asked, ignoring the TV and looking at me.

"A little harder than usual, but I've improved."

"You must be excited to eat again."

"It's usually the thing I miss the most." My hands came together, and I watched her green eyes convey her emotions throughout the conversation. She was easy to read because her emotions always seemed to be at the surface. She was excited about everything in life, never speaking in a monotone because she had too much passion. "How're you adjusting to the house?"

"No adjustment required. Torpedo and I both love it."

"How is he?" I hadn't seen him since I'd returned home.

"Good. Still sleeping on the couch even though he knows he's not supposed to. Same ol', same ol'."

I chuckled. "You can't get mad at him, though."

"No...not when he's the guy I'm sleeping with." She chuckled too.

Did that mean she was still single? Not that I should care... "How's work?"

"Good. In the last three months, I picked up so many shifts that I only had like...seven days off total."

"Wow."

"But I bought a house with it, so that's okay."

I liked that Charlotte was a hard worker. Most women I met weren't so ambitious, weren't willing to hustle for what they wanted. But then again, I was usually attracted to women who only cared about their looks...which meant they lacked in other departments. "It's a big accomplishment. You should be proud."

"Oh, I'm so proud. It's one of those things I brag about any chance I get."

"It's true," Stacy said. "She hasn't shut up about it."

"Just like how you never shut up about being pregnant," Char jabbed.

Stacy rolled her eyes. "Touché..."

―――――

WHEN THE GAME WAS OVER, we said goodbye and entered the hallway.

I left when Charlotte left, looking for an opportunity to talk to her when Vic and Stacy weren't around.

"Do you need a ride?" Charlotte asked. "Are you allowed to drive yet?"

"Yeah, the doctors cleared me."

We walked down the hallway, took the elevator to the bottom floor, and then left the lobby to head to the parking lot. It was the first time we'd been alone since we'd been seeing each other, and I instantly missed the familiarity of it. It was the only time in my life that I had intimacy with a woman. I'd had more flings than I could count, but those were meaningless. This was actually real.

"Too bad. We actually kinda live close to each other, so it wouldn't have been out of my way."

"Well, if you want to drive me around all day, I'm not gonna say no."

She smiled as she walked to her truck. "I'm glad you're back. Maybe I shouldn't say this, but I was really worried about you. Last time I watched your capsule land in the ocean, I was just a mesmerized spectator. But now, I'm so involved, so concerned. I understand how Vic feels."

I wished my friends and family didn't worry about my well-being since I was willing to die for my work, but it did make my chest feel warm knowing that she was concerned for my safety, that she thought about me while I was away. "You shouldn't waste your time worrying. It gets you upset for no reason, and you shouldn't put yourself through that until there's something to really worry about."

"Ouch."

"I mean that generally."

"And I'll always worry about you, Neil." She reached her truck and crossed her arms over her chest. It was nighttime since the sun set much earlier than it had before my mission. Now her cutoff jeans were long gone, replaced by pants and t-shirts.

I slid my hands into the front of my jeans and knew I should walk to my car and drive away. But I stood there with her, without a conversation starter. She certainly felt like a friend, but she felt like more than that too. "What's new with you?"

"I told you about my house, dog, and my job. I'm not a famous astronaut, so my life isn't as interesting." She smiled, telling me that she was teasing me.

"I meant your personal life."

"Oh...there's not much to tell on that front either. I went on a couple dates, but they never went anywhere. What about you?"

"Not a lot of opportunity to date on the moon."

"I meant since you got home," she said with a chuckle.

"Oh. No." I shook my head because I hadn't tried to chase tail like I usually did. Anytime I returned home from one of my missions, pussy was the first thing on my mind, and it was easy to find. This time, the second I returned home, I went for my hand instead...which wasn't like me.

She stared at me blankly, as if she didn't believe me. "I saw Cameron a couple of weeks ago..."

"I'm sorry."

She smiled slightly.

"What did that asshole want?"

"I actually went to see him."

"Good. You've finally decided to punch him in the face."

"Not that either..." She leaned against the hood of her truck.

I stepped closer, watching her face under the streetlight.

"Stacy told me he and his girlfriend lost the baby..." Her smile disappeared, and now she looked miserable, like it was her baby that she lost. "I brought him flowers and told him how sorry I was... Just terrible."

It was terrible, pain no one should ever have to suffer. But I was still surprised she went out of her way to comfort him, to do anything nice when he didn't deserve it. That was the kind of person she was...innately kind. She was there for people when they weren't there for her. Her love was unconditional, and she didn't hold grudges...even though this one was a perfectly valid grudge to keep. "That is terrible."

"Kyle thought I was crazy for being kind to him. He cheated on me with that woman and knocked her up while we were still married. Kyle said it was karma. But I refuse to believe the universe works like that."

"I have to agree with Kyle for this one. Not the karma part, but everything else."

She continued to stare at me, her arms tight over her chest.

"I wonder if he's actually the problem instead of you."

She shook her head. "The doctors said it was me."

"Was he tested?"

"No...but they said I was barren."

"Maybe he's not so perfect either. Maybe this experience will make him realize how much of an asshole he was to you."

"Maybe...but I think he has bigger problems right now."

Cameron was a big fucking dumbass for letting Charlotte go, for having her forever and throwing her away. When things got tough, he jumped ship, and that made him less of a man. A real man wouldn't leave his woman—for any reason. If the same thing happened to Stacy, Vic would stay by her side. He would stay by her side no matter what—and love her unconditionally. This guy was a piece of shit. "You're kind to be sympathetic, but he doesn't deserve your sympathy. He failed you as a husband, and you deserve someone much better. You shouldn't be the one buying him flowers. He should be the one on his knees, begging for forgiveness."

She held my gaze without blinking, clearly having no idea what to say to that.

Just like in the past, we were having deep conversations, the types of conversations that didn't happen between platonic friends. There was something more here. It wasn't friendship, and it certainly wasn't lust.

Then, what was it?

When the silence stretched, she cleared her voice. "Well, I should get going. Torpedo will worry."

I didn't want her to go. I almost grabbed her wrist and asked her to stay, asked her to stand under that streetlight and talk for the rest of the night. I was lonely on the moon, but now I was even lonelier on Earth—because she was the only person I wanted to talk to. "Goodnight, Slurpee."

She smiled at the nickname. "Still going to call me that?" She unlocked the car door then opened it.

"Definitely."

7

CHARLOTTE

NEIL WAS JUST AS DREAMY AS I REMEMBERED.

Those brown eyes, strong shoulders, gorgeous smile...he had it all.

It was hard to be around him and behave like friends...real friends. It was hard not to wrap my arms around his neck and kiss him right under that streetlight. It was hard not to open my legs and ask him to fuck me all night long.

But somehow, I managed to pull it off.

Kyle walked me to my truck after our shift at the hospital. We maneuvered down the aisles of cars, moving to the very rear where our vehicles were located. It was almost six in the evening because we both had to work late. Orders got backed up, so we stayed an extra hour to help out.

Kyle was close to my side, his shoulder rubbing against mine from time to time. "What are your plans tonight?"

"I don't know. Probably sitting on the couch with my dog."

"Sounds nice to me."

"Torpedo is a great cuddler."

"Can I join you?"

I turned to him. "You want to cuddle with my dog?"

He chuckled. "No. I want to cuddle with you."

I did a double take. "What?"

"I mean, I want to come over and sit on the couch with you. Is that cool?"

I didn't have any other plans. It wasn't like Neil was going to come over and rock my world. Maybe he was rocking someone else's world tonight. "Sure, why not?"

"Cool. You want me to grab beer on the way?"

"I have plenty."

"Even better." He walked to his truck and got inside.

When I made it to mine, my phone rang. It was Stacy. "Hey, girl. I already invited Kyle over, but you guys are welcome to tag along."

"Actually, I'm calling to talk about something important."

"Alright. If you're going to ask me to be your baby's godmother, you know my answer is yes."

"No, not that. Come on, you think I'd ask you that over the phone?"

"I don't know. Do we need to do anything dramatic when we talk every single day?"

"Probably not, but come on, I'm more romantic than that."

I chuckled. "Could you imagine if Kyle heard us right now? His head would explode."

"I know, right?" she said. "But what I'm about to say is pretty serious."

"Alright…" A part of me hoped it was about Neil, that maybe he said he missed me or something. It was a stupid fantasy, I knew that. But a girl could dream, right?

"Cameron called me."

Oh Jesus. "Why?"

"He said he went to your old apartment, but you weren't there."

Why didn't he just call? Why did he want to talk to me at all?

"He was persistent, so I gave him your new address. Hope that's okay."

If Stacy didn't give it to him, he would have found out some other way. "No, it's fine. I have no idea what he wants to talk about, especially in person."

"Maybe you're going to get a long-overdue apology. Or even better, he's gonna try to get you back."

"Why would that be even better?"

"That's the ultimate fantasy," she said. "When your ex begs you to take him back, and you shut the door in his face."

That wasn't a fantasy of mine anymore. I'd rather just skip that whole thing. "God, I hope that doesn't happen. His girlfriend just lost their baby, and that would be such an asshole move if he came after me."

"He's an asshole, so I wouldn't put it past him."

"I really hope you're wrong." I turned on the engine and pulled out of the parking lot. "Thanks for the heads-up. Hopefully, he just wants to apologize."

"Yeah...hopefully."

TORPEDO TOOK up an entire couch by himself because he was such a big dog that stretched out his paws in every direction. His eyes were closed, and his belly rose and fell with his deep breathing, an occasional snort coming out.

That meant Kyle and I had to share one couch. His arm was over the back of the cushions as he sat beside me, his eyes on Torpedo. "I thought he wasn't supposed to be on the couch?"

I rolled my eyes. "I give up."

He chuckled. "Maybe that's for the best."

We watched the game together, talking about the stupid calls the refs made as well as the players. Some were injured, and that was greatly affecting the score. I drank a light beer, and when the bottle was empty, I left it on the table beside me.

"Want me to grab you another one?" he asked.

"No. I've had enough beer for one evening." I glanced at my dog on the other couch then kept watching the game. The winning team was so far ahead in the score, there was no chance the other team could catch up. Made the game a bit boring.

Kyle's hand rested against the back of my neck, and I suddenly felt his fingers move under my hairline. The touch was so subtle, so soft, I thought I made the whole thing up. But his fingers dug deeper and deeper, and soon he was rubbing the back of my neck harder.

I tensed at his touch, not repulsed by it, just shocked.

His fingers grabbed the curtain of hair covering my cheek and pulled it over my shoulder, exposing my neck and face.

The hairs up and down my arms stood on end. My heart started to race. Time slowed down around me, and while my eyes were still on the game, I wasn't even watching it. I was aware Kyle was touching me, touching me the exact same way he used to during our short fling. Unsure what else to do, I sat there, rigid as a statue.

He moved his face closer to mine, his blue eyes drilling into my face like he was demanding my attention, commanding me to look at him the same way.

My heart was pounding against my rib cage, making my entire body shake. My fingertips were numb.

His hand slid to the back of my head, cupping it like he intended to guide my face where he wanted it. Then he slowly forced me to look at him, to lock on to his gaze head on.

I looked into his blue eyes, bright like the sky, and felt time stand still.

His eyes glanced down to my lips, making his intentions crystal clear.

I had the chance to turn away, to end this before it even began. But like a deer in the headlights, I did nothing. I felt the adrenaline circulate in my veins, felt the temperature of my body rise by several degrees.

When there was no objection, Kyle went for it. He leaned in, cradled the back of my head, and kissed me.

It'd been almost a year since the last time this happened, the last time he kissed me in my old apartment. He was a good kisser then, and he still was one now. His fingertips lightly touched my hair and gradually turned possessive. His kiss was subtle in the beginning, just a simple peck, but once I reciprocated, it turned deeper.

I kissed him back, lulled by the comfort. I always knew Kyle was a good-looking guy. He was muscular and fit with a handsome face, but all those perks were swallowed by our friendship. I didn't see him in that way, even though we'd screwed and he made me come each time. But I'd known it wasn't right, that I wasn't in a good place for anything physical or romantic. I had been trying to forget about Cameron, to make myself feel better.

But this was different.

Kyle slowly guided me down against the couch, moving on top of me and maneuvering between my thighs at the same time. He kissed me good, so good that I almost forgot how wrong this was.

My head hit the pillow, and my fingers gripped his biceps. His kiss wasn't like Neil's, the man who was on my mind most of the time. He was the man I wanted but could never have, and a three-month hiatus hadn't made me forget him. But it was nice to forget him about for a few moments. My thighs squeezed his hips, and I opened my mouth so I could take his tongue.

He moaned into my mouth.

While it felt good, I knew it was the same thing as last time.

I was trying to forget about Cameron before, and now I was trying to forget about Neil. Maybe Kyle had too many beers and he just wanted something physical. Maybe he just wanted to get laid and have a one-night stand. Or maybe this meant something more. Either way, this wasn't a good idea. I valued our friendship far too much to use him. I'd done it once, and I wouldn't do it again. "Kyle..." I turned my mouth away from his and pressed my palms against his chest.

He stayed on top of me, his body still as he pressed me into the cushions. It seemed like he wouldn't move, that he would seduce me until he got what he wanted. But then pragmatism set in, and he moved off me.

My heart was still racing a million miles an hour as I sat up. I fixed my hair and avoided eye contact, embarrassed when he was probably the one who was embarrassed. "I'm sorry... I just don't think it's a good idea."

"Why not?" His deep voice filled the silence between us. "You're obviously attracted to me."

"That doesn't mean this is a good idea. We're friends, Kyle."

"What if I want to be more than friends?"

I turned my face back to him, taking in the sight of his shining blue eyes.

"You've been divorced almost a year. You're in a good place. It's time you try again."

"What are you saying, Kyle? Are you looking for sex? Or a relationship?"

He held my look for a long time as he considered his response. "Whatever you want, Char. I'm tired of seeing you date these loser guys, sleep with them even though you don't like them very much—"

"And you don't do the exact same thing?" I snapped. "That's sexist, Kyle."

"That's not at all what I meant. I just meant, if you're looking for good sex, I'm right here." He placed his hand across his chest. "If you're ready to date, I'm first in line. You could keep wasting time with losers, or you could be with a real man. That's all I'm saying."

Now I wondered if I'd been reading Kyle wrong all this time. "This is a lot to take in..."

"It doesn't have to be."

I turned my gaze back to the game but didn't watch it.

"I'm not like Cameron, and I'm not like Neil. I will be here for you every single day. When bad shit happens, I'm not gonna take off like Cameron, and I won't jump into a rocket like Neil. I can be exactly what you deserve—if you give me a chance."

My hands covered my face, and I slowly dragged them down my cheeks. "I thought we were just friends..."

"We are friends, Char."

"But I thought that was all we were..."

"My friendship with you is real. If you don't want me, I'm still gonna be here. But I think you do want me, and I'm tired of being in the friend zone. I moved too fast when you got divorced, and I realize that was an idiotic mistake. I just knew you wouldn't be single for long, so I had to do something sooner rather than later... Looking back, I realize I should have been a friend and nothing more. But now, you're seeing guys, and you're in a good place. It's time for me to do something before someone else takes my spot. I'm sorry to make you uncomfortable, but I'd rather take my shot and get rejected than hate myself for waiting too long."

I was overloaded with information, so I sat there in silence, unsure what to do or what to say.

"Like I said, there's chemistry here."

"Maybe you're just a good kisser…"

"If you think I'm a good kisser, then there's chemistry here. If you're attracted to me, there's chemistry. Both of those are true."

All of this felt overwhelming. I started to breathe heavily because I was scared, scared I was about to lose another person in my life. If I rejected him, it would be awkward forever. If I dated him and we broke up, we would never be friends again. Losing Cameron left a huge void in my life, not because of the way he hurt me, but because he wasn't there anymore. I couldn't afford to lose anyone else.

"What's wrong?" Kyle knew me so well.

"Yes, I'm attracted to you. Yes, I liked sleeping with you in the past. But I think it's best if we just stay friends…"

Silence. Painful silence.

Minutes later, he spoke. "Look at me."

That was the last thing I wanted to do.

"Now."

I turned back to him.

"Tell me why."

"Because you mean too much to me. I would never want to lose you. When people date, they break up. And when they break up, they can never stand to be in the same room together. I can't let that happen."

"What if we don't break up?"

"We will."

He shook his head slightly. "Cameron was an asshole. I'm not an asshole."

"I know that."

"Then give me some credit. I've spent the last year waiting for the perfect moment to swoop in. You obviously mean something to me."

"And I thought Cameron and I would be together for the rest of our lives. We were stupidly in love, calling each other soul mates. Couples think they'll last forever, but most of them don't. I love you too much to take the gamble, Kyle. I'm sorry to hurt you...I really am. But I don't think it's a good idea."

He bowed his head and sighed loudly.

"Besides...I still have feelings for Neil."

He raised his head slowly, his dark eyes watching me.

"So even if I weren't scared about losing you, it still wouldn't be right. I would just be using you to stop thinking about someone else, and I couldn't do that to you. I love you too much. Sleeping with a random guy is different because there's no chance of anyone getting hurt."

He watched me for several heartbeats. "What if I don't care?"

"Well, I do."

"They say the best way to get over someone is to get under someone else. Trust me, I can make you forget about him."

"I told you I wouldn't use you like that, Kyle."

He sighed in annoyance and looked away.

The tense silence returned, a nice evening ruined by what happened. I was flattered Kyle wanted me because he was handsome, hardworking, and a man who could get any woman he wanted. But he meant too much for me to lose. Now I was afraid that had happened anyway...that this friendship was over. "I really hope this doesn't change anything between us...because I love you."

He lifted his gaze and looked at me again, the anger slowly disappearing from the surface of his eyes. When he sighed, it was a much quieter tone. His hands relaxed from the fists he had made. "No...nothing ever could."

"WHAT'S WRONG?" Stacy stopped eating her salad so she could interrogate me.

Our lunch breaks were at the same time, so we decided to meet up at our favorite healthy spot. "What makes you think anything is wrong?"

"Because there's something wrong."

Kyle and I were working together that day, and while it was tense in the beginning, he behaved like he normally would, saying the same things he always said. He made an effort to keep everything the same, so it wasn't as bad as I'd imagined it would be. Maybe in time, last night would just be a bad memory.

"What is it?" She sipped her water and narrowed her eyes on my face.

"Well...Kyle came over last night."

"And?"

"He made a move on me."

She was about to stab a strawberry with her fork, but instead, she lifted her gaze and looked at me again. "He did?"

"He kissed me. I let it go on for a bit before I came to my senses."

"Came to your senses?" she mocked. "Kyle is super-hot. Why wouldn't you want to tap that?"

"Because we're friends."

"So?" she snapped. "Friends become lovers all the time."

"And lovers break up and stop being friends."

She rolled her eyes. "That doesn't happen to everyone. Vic and I will be together until we die."

"I'm sure you will...you're one of the lucky ones."

She gave me a sad look. "Char, I think you're making a mistake rejecting Kyle."

"I disagree."

"He adores you. That guy would never hurt you, not in a million years."

"And what if I hurt him?" I countered. "What if I screw it up and ruin everything?"

"You wouldn't."

"We don't know that. I doubt Cameron ever thought he would do something so terrible. The villain never thinks they're the villain."

Stacy sighed. "You seriously need to let this Cameron thing go."

"I have. I just don't think risking a solid friendship is the way to go about it."

"Char, you need to—"

"I still have feelings for Neil." I was tired of keeping that information to myself and not sharing my deepest emotions with my best friend. I was embarrassed I still cared about the man who had been gone for three months. I should have gotten over him, but I never did. I was still in the exact same place. "I told Kyle that. I would never want him to be a substitute for the man I actually want…"

Now that Stacy knew the truth, she stopped applying the pressure. She stared at me with eyes wide open, and then slowly, she let a long breath escape her lips as the rest of her body deflated.

I'd intended to hold that secret until my feelings faded away, but I suspected they may never fade away. Neil was gone for three months with zero communication, but I was still in the same place emotionally. That meant pursuing a physical relationship would be even stupider. My heart was inflated with all these feelings…which meant it was more likely to be popped. There wasn't a chance we would have a happy ending. It was certain he would break my heart...and that meant it would be idiotic to go down that road.

Stacy kept staring at me. "I thought it was just a meaningless fling?"

"It was..."

"Then how can you still feel this way? Are you hooking up again?"

"No." I wished we were.

"You guys didn't talk for three months."

"I know..."

She pushed her salad aside and rested her elbows on the table. "Does he know?"

I shook my head. "I would never tell him. We agreed to be friends, and it'll stay that way."

"Then maybe you should move on with someone else."

"Using Kyle isn't the answer, Stacy. That's not fair."

"Kyle wouldn't care."

No, he wouldn't. "That's beside the point."

She kept staring at me, clearly annoyed by the situation.

"Why are you angry?"

"Because I knew it was a mistake for the two of you to hook up in the first place."

"I don't regret it."

"Well, I do," she snapped. "I watched Cameron break your heart, and I don't want to watch Neil do the same thing. He's a great guy, loyal and hardworking, but he's a playboy. He's unavailable. You do understand that a relationship with Neil only ends one way, right?"

"Yes..."

"Then you need to forget about him and move on. I suggest you move on with Kyle. When we hang out, we can only go to your place, that way you never have to see Neil. We can cut him out of your life without cutting him out of ours."

"That's unnecessary. I said I still have feelings for him, not that I'm in love with him." I just missed his affection, the way he felt on top of me and inside me. The sex was good, and the talking was even better. It felt comfortable and nerve-racking at the same time.

"If you still think about him like this, then it sounds like you're on that path."

I stared at my half-eaten salad.

Stacy stared at me for a long time before she sighed. "I don't understand you. Kyle is the perfect guy. He's got a good job, he owns a house, he's gorgeous, he's fit...and he adores you."

I already knew all those things. Under different circumstances, he would probably be the guy I fell in love with. If I'd met him before Cameron, I probably would have married him instead.

"You say you don't want to get hurt again... Kyle is the answer."

"I don't want to risk losing him."

"You risk losing him no matter what. He could end up with someone else, and she could hate you because you slept with him a long time ago. You guys drift apart and stop talking altogether."

"Kyle would never let that happen…"

"Then what are you scared of?"

"Breaking up is different. Look at Cameron and me. You think we'll ever be friends?"

"I don't know," she said with a shrug. "He did knock up some other woman, and you brought him flowers when he lost the baby."

"That's not the same thing…"

"I think you and Kyle have a strong connection and incredible respect for each other. I doubt you would ever break up, and if you did, you would both make an effort to keep your friendship. You already slept together and bounced back from that."

"Not the same thing…"

"Fine," she snapped. "You rejected him, and the next day everything was still normal."

I didn't have an argument against that.

"Forget about Neil. Go after Kyle."

"I can't just forget about Neil. If I could, I would have done that by now. Neil and I… There's just this connection. I can't explain. Anytime I'm around him, I feel like I'm floating… It's just so easy."

She still wasn't sympathetic. "Girl, forget about him. Otherwise, you'll end up like all the others…heartbroken and forgotten. He's incredible successfully and so damn charming, he makes every woman feel this way. You're just another notch on his bedpost. You mean nothing to him, Char. I hate to put it like that, to be so cold, but that's the truth."

It was hard to hear, and I still didn't believe it. Maybe Neil didn't feel anything for me at all, but I knew I didn't mean nothing. I knew he would always care about me...at least as a friend.

———

WHEN I PULLED up to the house, Torpedo was looking out the window as he stood on the back of the couch. He was barking loudly, but normally, he would be lying on the floor pretending to be a good boy when he heard the garage door open. So this behavior was unusual.

That was when I noticed Cameron step out of his car onto the sidewalk.

Oh shit.

I pulled into the garage, turned off the car, and took a deep breath as I prepared for whatever was about to happen.

I got out and walked to the driveway, seeing him standing there in a t-shirt and dark jeans. He'd always been fit because he was blessed by the universe, maintaining his fitness without doing much to earn it. He had toned arms and a flat stomach that always showed the outline of his abs. He looked at me apologetically, like he felt bad for being there at all.

I crossed my arms over my chest and stopped in front of him. "What are you doing here, Cameron?" When I'd dropped off those flowers, my intentions were pure. I wasn't engaging in some psychological warfare. I genuinely wanted to comfort him during this difficult time, even though he had been fucking someone else when he should have been comforting me.

"I didn't mean to creep you out by waiting for you to come home. I stopped by because I thought you would be off work by now, and when you didn't show up, I thought you were running late or something..."

Seeing him parked in front of my house wasn't the issue. It was the fact that he was there at all. "What are you doing here, Cameron?" If he needed something, a phone call was sufficient. The fact that he asked Stacy for my address was a little concerning. I hoped he just wanted to give an apology and nothing more.

He slid his hands into his front pockets and looked at me with trepidation. "I've been doing a lot of thinking, and...I feel like shit for everything that happened between us. I've always wanted a family, and when I didn't get my way, I acted like such an asshole. I treated you like an oven more than a person...more than my wife...and I'm so sorry." His eyes lowered to the concrete below his feet like he couldn't look at me anymore. "I'm ashamed of my behavior, ashamed of the man I am. You were just as devastated as I was, and I shouldn't have turned my back on you like that... I shouldn't have talked to Vivian online and snuck around behind your back. I have so many things to apologize for, and as I say it, I realize how insufficient an apology is. How could I ever apologize for something so heinous? So horrific?" He kept his eyes on the ground and took a deep breath. Moisture coated the surface of his gaze, and he sniffed as he inhaled the mucus back into his nose. "I'm still comforting Vivian right now, but I told her we couldn't be together anymore— not because she lost the baby, but because looking at her reminds me of what I did." He finally lifted his gaze to look into mine. "I'm so sorry, Char. I know this probably means nothing to you, but I wanted you to know that."

It was hard to hold a grudge when he seemed so sincere, when my compassion made him reflect on his own lack of it. I hadn't seen him cry once in our relationship, except when his father died, and watching him shed tears now made me feel his sincerity. "I forgive you, Cameron."

His tears steadied as he stared at me, like he couldn't believe what I just said. "You shouldn't."

"You know me, I can never stay mad at anybody."

He smiled slightly, his eyes still wet. "I can't believe I was so stupid. I was married to the most amazing woman in the world, and I fucked it up. When the doctors told us you were barren, my mind snapped, and I just lost it. It was so difficult that I spun out of control and did idiotic stuff. I cheated on you, divorced you, and disposed of you like you were nothing. I just want you to know that everything before...that was all real. I did love you. I was happy with you. It's no excuse, but hearing the terrible news was so traumatic that I changed."

I believed that because I had been there. We were happy together. People often said we were meant to be. "I know..."

He shook his head and sighed. "I think what happened with Vivian was the universe punishing me—"

"Don't say that, Cameron. That's not true. No one deserves that—no matter what."

"See?" he whispered. "You're so...unbelievably kind."

"Anyone would say the same, Cameron." And if they didn't, they were evil.

He stared at me for a while, his hands remaining in his pockets. Silence stretched for a long time because there was nothing to say now that he apologized. Tensions and emotions lingered between us.

I thought I should say goodbye and enter the house, but that seemed cold. The conversation wasn't over, even though there was nothing to say.

"Are you still dating that astronaut?" he whispered.

So Cameron had recognized him. "No. We're just friends."

"Oh...is he an idiot too?"

"No." I am.

He continued to stare at me. "Are you dating anyone?"

Just boring guys that I immediately forgot about. "No."

He nodded slightly. "I'm surprised."

"After everything that happened between us, I haven't been eager to start a relationship. I've been taking it easy... keeping it casual."

His eyes filled with sadness once again, knowing he was responsible for my lingering heartbreak. "I doubt there's any guy out there dumber than me, so you shouldn't keep your guard up."

I tightened my arms over my chest.

"I know this is stupid and premature, but I would love to maybe...get some coffee sometime."

I never imagined my ex-husband would appear in my driveway, apologize for hurting me, and then ask me out on a date. "Cameron, you literally just broke up with Vivian...the woman who lost your baby—"

"I'm not asking you on a date. I just want to talk. That's all."

"Still...Vivian is the only woman who should have your attention right now. You apologize to me for what you did, but here you are, doing the same thing. Vivian didn't give you what you wanted, so now you're dumping her and jumping on to the next thing..."

"That's not at all what's happening—"

"Seems that way to me."

He held up both hands, like that would somehow silence me. "Look, Vivian and I had our differences months ago. We agreed to stay together because of the kid. She and I rushed into things way too fast. We hardly knew each other when we got pregnant. She was practically a stranger to me. Now that we've lost the baby...the thing keeping us together doesn't exist anymore."

"But you would never have asked me to coffee if she hadn't lost the baby."

"I guess that's true...but not because of the reason you think. The only reason why I'm here, why I had this epiphany, is because you were there for me when I wasn't there for you. When you brought me those flowers, I realized I had been a total asshole to you. I realized I never deserved you. My blurred vision cleared, and everything hit me at once. I knew I shouldn't have left, I knew I had the greatest woman in the world who loved me...but I'd lost sight of that. The truth that I tried to deny came back to haunt me, and I changed. I literally changed in that moment. So...I'm not repeating my past mistakes. I'd be lying if I said I didn't want to get back together someday, that I want to get my wife back and adopt a few kids. But for right now...maybe we could just get coffee and be friends."

Cameron had been the love of my life. The years I spent with him were my happiest. Hearing him say everything I wanted to hear almost brought tears to my eyes. But the love I had for him wasn't strong enough to erase the past, to make me forget what he did. He could be as apologetic as he wanted, but it would never make me trust him again. "Cameron, we're never going to get back together."

He didn't blink, and his complexion suddenly turned pale.

"And I find it unlikely we could ever be friends."

He still didn't blink.

"I think we can be friendly to each other, wish each other the best in life, and say hello when we bump into each other at the grocery store. But that's it..." I didn't get any satisfaction out of this moment, didn't feel an ounce of revenge.

His eyes welled up with tears.

I hurt him...and I didn't feel good about it. "I'm sorry, Cameron."

When the tears started to streak down his face, he wiped them away with the back of his forearm. He sniffed loudly. "I would never hurt you again, Char. I promise. I know I did something really terrible—"

"I'm still broken, Cameron. I've been with a few guys, but I've been really persistent about being casual. I can't picture myself getting married again. I can't picture myself being in a relationship again. We were so happy together, and if you could do something like that...then no relationship will last.

I've lost my faith in love. I've lost my faith in relationships. So, I'm not looking for anything serious—with anyone. You want us to go back to what we were, but that's not possible because I'm not that person anymore. Your actions changed me, morphed me into a whole new person. We can't be married again, we can't be happy again, because neither one us is the person we used to be."

8

NEIL

I did three more reps before Vic helped me navigate the bar back to the rack.

"Not bad."

I sat up and wiped my forehead with a towel. "I'll build my strength back up in a couple of months."

"You really think it will take that long?"

"I was on the moon, where gravity is one-sixth that of Earth. Yeah...it'll take a while." I rose to my feet and let Vic take my place.

He lay down and picked up the bar and started to do his reps.

I kept an eye on him, just in case he needed me.

Vic pumped the weight on his large arms, sweat streaking down his forehead. The vein across his temple fattened with the exertion.

I kept count, and when he finished, I racked the weight. "Not bad."

"Shut up, I can do fifty pounds more than you." He sat up and wiped his forehead with the towel.

"For now."

"Whatever, I've always been bigger than you."

"But no stronger. Big difference."

He grabbed his jug of water and took a large drink. The sound of weights clanking against metal filled the gym, along with the loud music that no one was listening to because they were all listening to their own music.

A pretty blonde in leggings and a sports bra walked up to my brother, confident because she sported a perfect body with a belly button piercing. "Hey." With both hands on her hips, she gave him a flirtatious smile before she hit on him. "You know, I could use some help. Want to give me a hand?"

My brother gave the same reaction he gave to all interested woman. He was visibly annoyed and ice-cold. "I'm married." He held up his left hand, where a black wedding ring contrasted against his fair skin. "Don't hit on a married man. One day, you'll be married, and you'll hope some chick at the gym doesn't hit on him." He flipped his towel over his shoulder and walked off to the next machine.

The woman stood there in shock, as if she couldn't believe any man would blow her off like that. She was probably used to getting any guy she wanted.

I tried not to smile. My brother didn't put on that act for my benefit. He knew I would take his secrets to the grave. If he had an affair, I would keep my mouth shut. But his response to interested women was always the same. He was indifferent to all of them, attracted to only one woman in the world—his wife. He had a haughty attitude, a constant asshole-ish personality. That came from his profession, being an aggressive litigator who was ruthless in the courthouse. He had no time for bullshit, and to him, hitting on a married man was bullshit.

When she was finally recovered, she turned to me. "Well, I could still use some help..."

I didn't mind swooping in and taking the women who were interested in him before me, but her looks didn't appeal to me. I didn't picture myself gripping her blond hair then spanking her ass. There was no attraction at all, even though there was nothing wrong with her. "I'm taken too."

"Of course...the hot ones usually are."

I joined my brother at the next machine. "You know, you don't have to be a *complete* asshole every time a woman hits on you."

"She knew I was married."

"Maybe she didn't."

"Trust me, if a guy wears a ring, a woman notices." He picked up the weights off the ground and slid them onto the rack.

"Still don't see why you need to be so cold. A simple no would suffice."

"It just bothers me, alright?" He picked up another plate and slid it onto the pole.

"Care to share?"

He finished getting the rack ready for our workout then turned to me. With one arm resting over the rack, he put the other hand on his hips. "I wouldn't want some handsome guy hitting on my wife. I wouldn't want some rich, good-looking dude to sweep her off her feet and take her away from me. I wish people would just respect marriage so that never happens."

I forced myself not to smile because teasing him about his insecurity would be mean. My brother had always been hard and ruthless, being a macho guy who didn't have issues. But deep down underneath, he was insecurities like everyone else. "No one could ever take Stacy away from you. So maybe tone down the dickishness."

"I am a dick. It's nothing something I can change. Why didn't you go out with her?"

I shrugged. "Not interested."

"Why not?"

"What do you mean, why not? Sometimes you're interested, and sometimes you aren't."

"But you're *always* interested, Neil."

I shrugged again because I didn't know what to say. I'd been home for several weeks now and there had been plenty of opportunity for pussy, but I never took it. My short conversations with Charlotte were far more fulfilling. "I guess it's taking me some time to get used to normal life again."

"When you get back to Earth, you're like a sailor on leave. What's different this time?" Instead of getting into position to do his squats, he kept talking to me over the sound of music and loud machines.

I pictured her green eyes, soft lips, and the way her hair rested on my pillow. It was hard not to picture her face throughout the day, to be at work and working on the newest shuttle without daydreaming about the little brunette and her lazy dog.

My brother kept watching me with his hostile gaze. "There's something you aren't telling me."

"You're reading too much into it."

"No, I'm not. You're behaving the way I do. Except I'm married, and you aren't. That means there's someone in your life. Who is she?"

"You're jumping to conclusions."

"Am I?" he countered. "Go back to the blonde and ask her out."

"I'm not gonna pick up a woman just to prove a point."

"Any other time, you would." His skills as a lawyer were his greatest asset in an argument. He was always right, even if he was wrong. It was stupid to go against him, especially when he was right...and he was definitely right in this situation. "We aren't only brothers, we are friends. So why don't you just man up and explain yourself?"

I held his gaze and tried to think of a way to express myself. I wasn't entirely sure how I felt, so sharing that information with someone else was challenging.

"Well?" he pressed.

I finally caved. "I still have a thing for Charlotte..."

Vic's eyes narrowed in annoyance. He'd probably assumed there was some other chick in my life, someone I wasn't ready to talk about yet. He had always been protective of Charlotte, treating her like a little sister rather than a friend of his wife's. His eyes were immediately hostile.

"I keep thinking about her, so I haven't really been interested in other women. I didn't realize how bad it was until you pointed it out." I wasn't going out to bars and picking up women the way I used to. More importantly, when women came to me, I still didn't take the bait. I was celibate without any clear explanation.

Vic still stared at me, that haunting gaze a little terrifying.

"I can tell you aren't happy with that response..."

"I thought you and Char were long over."

"We are over."

"Then why do you feel this way? You've been gone for three months. Are you still screwing?"

"No. We're just friends—like we agreed on."

He lowered his arm from the rack then came closer to me, halting his workout altogether. "How can you feel this way after being gone for so long?"

I shrugged. "Not sure. Every time I talk to her, I just...enjoy it."

He grabbed the towel off his shoulder and patted his forehead again. "Neil..." He wrapped it around the back of his neck to absorb the sweat that dripped from his scalp down to his back. "Don't go down that road again. She needs something stable. She needs a man who's always going to be around."

Kyle popped into my head. "Nothing is going to happen. She doesn't seem interested in me anymore."

"What makes you say that?"

I shrugged. "I don't know...it just doesn't seem like it."

"Charlotte is a really amazing woman. I have no idea why Cameron flipped out, because he had the perfect life. Even if she can't have children, she's still twice the woman than any other chick he could possibly find. She deserves the best, a man who's gonna put her back together and never break her. No offense, man, but that's not you. You had a short-term fling, and it's over. Don't go down that road again."

"Wow...didn't realize you had such a low opinion of me."

"I don't have a low opinion of you. I think you're a great man, and I couldn't be prouder. But you told me you'll never get married or have children. You'll always be dedicated to your job, and I respect that. But that means the only thing you can offer Charlotte is heartbreak. I'm just looking out for her. She's family to me. I don't care if you guys want to fool around and use each other, but I don't want Charlotte to get hurt. I don't think she's capable of having a long-term fling without getting attached. I know her pretty well."

That was the reason I hadn't told Charlotte how I felt. As much as I wanted her in my bed again, I didn't want to hurt her. She said she didn't want to lose me, and the best way to do that was by staying friends. I also had no idea how she felt about me. Three months was a long time, and she'd probably gone weeks without even thinking about me. "The last thing I want to do is hurt you. You and I share the same sentiment."

"Good. Then forget about her." He turned back to the weights like the conversation was over.

"And how do you just forget someone?"

He turned back around. "You can start by taking that blonde home."

I sat in my living room and looked out the back window, imagining Torpedo lying in the grass under the tree. It was almost dark, so he wouldn't need the shade anyway. The TV was on, but I ignored it.

After my conversation with Vic, I went back to the blonde to make a move.

But I just couldn't do it.

I couldn't force myself to be with a woman I didn't want.

Fuck, I wanted Charlotte.

Now, my phone was in my hand, and I was considering texting her. Even if I couldn't be physical with her, I just wanted to be with her. We could spend the night making fun of Torpedo while drinking Slurpees, and I would be happy. Horny, but happy.

I gave in and texted her. *I'm in the neighborhood and realized I haven't seen your new place. Can I stop by?* It was such a lame excuse, but I couldn't say what I wanted outright. Being with other women was much easier because I could be straight-forward about my desires. But with Charlotte, I had to stick to the friend zone, which meant I had to behave like a buddy.

The three dots lit up on the screen before her reply appeared. *Sure! =)*

I PULLED up to the house then rang the doorbell.

My heart was beating so fucking fast. This girl made me nervous, which was saying something because I'd launched into space with millions of pounds of explosive rocket fuel without letting my heart rate exceed eighty beats per minute.

She opened the door, wearing tiny little pajama shorts and a white tank top. Unfortunately, she wore a bra, so I couldn't see her sexy nipples and the natural roundness of her tits. "You got here fast. You must have been close—" She was pushed out of the way as Torpedo sprinted past her then jumped on me.

"Whoa, boy." I laughed as his front paw smacked against my stomach as he rose on his hind legs. He barked then let his tongue hang out of his mouth as he looked at me, like he'd missed me the entire time I was gone. "I missed you too, man." I rubbed him behind the ears and let him use me as a crutch.

"Oh my god, I'm so sorry. He's never done that before." She grabbed him by the collar. "Torpedo, down."

He obeyed but issued a quiet whine in protest.

A feeling of longing ran over me, a sensation of homesickness. This was what I missed most while I was on the moon. It wasn't my family or my friends. It was this beautiful girl and her dog.

She dragged him inside. "Don't embarrass me like that again."

"He's fine." I chuckled as I let myself inside and shut the door behind me. "Honestly, no one ever hugs me like that when I get home. It's nice."

She rolled her eyes. "Thanks for being so nice about it. He usually has better manners than that." She picked up a toy and set it on his blanket on the couch. "Come on, get up here."

He hopped up, his tail still wagging.

"Play with your toy and relax." She turned around and came back to me. "Alright, where were we before you got charged by a beast?"

Her green eyes were bright with a zest for life, and her ponytail kept all the hair off her beautiful face. She didn't wear makeup since she was prepared to stay in for the night, but a gorgeous woman like her didn't need any of that crap. She was stunning entirely on her own. It was hard not to stare, not to fantasize about what I could be doing to her that very moment.

"Neil?"

I'd been zoning out for a long time. "Sorry, I'm still recovering from that hit."

She chuckled then turned to her living room. "Well, this is the main room. It's all my old furniture, but it has a lot more room."

"Yeah, it's really nice. Looks like you got a new TV."

"I had to. The old one got smashed during the move."

"Yikes."

She shrugged. "I needed a new TV anyway, so I upgraded and got a bigger one. This room is so much larger than the living room in my apartment that I needed a large screen." She walked forward and entered the dining area. "I can have five people over for dinner, so that's cool."

"Very nice." I watched her walk into the kitchen, loving the way those little shorts practically showed her ass cheeks.

"This is the kitchen. I've got tons of counter space so I can cook a feast."

"You're welcome to cook me dinner anytime."

She chuckled then walked down the hallway. "A boring hall-way...no big deal. These are the two guest bedrooms, the bathroom, and then my master suite." She opened the door and stepped inside, showing her white dressers and bedframe and the pink bedspread on her mattress. "I've got more space in here, so that's nice too."

It was a major improvement to her apartment and suited her much better. But all I could think about was the last time we were on that bed together, our sweaty bodies writhing in passion. I wondered if she'd had another man in that bed since I'd been gone. I didn't dare ask. "I really like it."

"I like it too." She walked back into the hallway and entered the living room. "And that concludes the grand tour."

"You did an excellent job."

"You want a beer or anything? I've got some IPAs in the fridge."

"No, I'm okay." I was trying to bulk up and get my old

strength back, which meant cutting calories, especially from things like beer. I took a seat on the couch and saw that she had a preseason basketball game on.

"Suit yourself." She got one for herself and took the seat beside me.

On the other couch was Torpedo, who was staring at me anxiously with his toy in his mouth, quietly begging me to join him.

"He's giving you the guilt trip," she said. "Just ignore him."

"Is that possible?"

"It's hard in the beginning, but you get used to it. So, what's going on with you?" She crossed her legs, her shorts rising up a few extra inches with the movement. She brought the mouth of the bottle to her lips and took a drink.

Everything she did distracted me, from her sexy legs to those plump lips as they sealed around the bottle. "I've been working a lot."

"That's ridiculous, considering what you just did."

"There's just as much work that needs to be done as up there. And I've been hitting the gym with Vic."

"Why?"

"Getting back into shape."

"You look like you're in perfect shape to me," she blurted.

She treated me like I was nothing more than a friend, but the compliment suggested otherwise...or maybe that was just wishful thinking. "Thanks, but I always lose muscle mass during my missions. Lesser gravity creates lesser resistance for our muscles, so they atrophy. When I return to

Earth, the first few months are about protein shakes and exercise."

"That sounds like a lot of work."

"Being in shape makes the launches easier. I'm usually pretty strong for the first six weeks, so working is easier. Vic has been coming with me since he's a meathead."

"A meat what?"

"It means a beefy guy who's at the gym all the time."

"Oh, gotcha. It's nice that you guys spend some time together."

"Yeah...it is nice." We talked about work, women, and beer. "A woman made a pass at him, and he was such a dick to her. Sometimes it's fun to watch, and sometimes I just feel bad for the girls."

"He doesn't wear his wedding ring to the gym?"

"No, he does."

"Then why are women hitting on him?"

I guess she shared the same viewpoint as my brother. "I don't think they care."

"Gross." She took a drink from her beer. "Vivian slept with Cameron knowing full well he was married. I know I should only be mad at Cameron, but it's still disgusting to sleep with someone else's husband. I could never do something like that..."

Her integrity made her more desirable. "I've never seen my brother so committed to a woman. They've been married for years, but he's still just as involved now as he was then."

"That's so romantic... Stacy is so lucky. After everything that happened with Cameron, I lost all faith in men, marriage, and relationships. But Vic makes me believe true love is still out there... It's just extremely rare."

"It is out there, Char. Cameron was just a mistake."

She took a long drink of her beer then set it on the table next to her. Her eyes were on the TV for a long time, like she was thinking about something deeply. "He came by a couple of nights ago..."

"Cameron?" I asked, skeptical.

She nodded. "He apologized to me. Said he felt terrible for everything that happened."

"At least he admits he was an asshole."

"Yeah...I guess he and Vivian are going their separate ways. They were staying together because of the baby."

I already knew where this was going. Cameron apologized, and then he made a move. He finally realized he was a goddamn idiot who threw away the perfect woman. I hoped she didn't say yes...and not just for my own selfish reasons. "What did you say when he asked to get back together?"

She turned her face toward me. "What makes you assume that?"

"If he came to his senses and apologized, that means he's not stupid anymore. And if he's not stupid anymore, of course, he's gonna do everything he can to get you back."

She watched me for a while before she turned away. "Well... you're right."

"And your response?"

"Come on, you really think I would have said yes?" She turned back to me, a little disgruntled by the assumption.

"I didn't assume anything. That's why I asked."

She pivoted her body toward me, both of her legs coming into contact with my left one. "I loved that man so much. I'd have done anything for him in a heartbeat. I thought we would be together forever, but even though he seemed so sincere, that wasn't enough. He broke my trust, and once trust is broken, it can never be repaired. I told him I didn't want to be friends either. I don't want to be anything."

That was a relief, not just because I wanted her myself. I didn't want her to be with a man who treated her like trash. I wanted her to be someone who adored her, to be with a man like Vic...someone who would be faithful no matter what. "You made the right decision."

"Yeah, but it still didn't feel good. I didn't get any satisfaction or revenge. It hurt to hurt him."

"Because that's the kind of person you are..." She was too good to hold grudges, too saintly for revenge. The woman didn't have a mean bone in her body. Her heart was too pure for evil.

"I hope he falls in love again, and this time, he's the man he should have been with me."

I didn't possess her good heart or her compassion. I was cold and unforgiving. I understood good and evil—and nothing else. Perhaps my time in the military made me that way. But I didn't think Cameron deserved happiness, even after he apologized. What he did was still disgusting. What kind of man cheats on his wife after he finds out she's barren? As if he had every right to do what he wanted because she couldn't give him what he wanted. She wasn't livestock that he bought from a farm.

"Anyway…that's what's new with me." She ran her fingers through her ponytail, pulling it to one side to expose her shoulder. She had the softest skin, the kind that could be kissed for hours as foreplay. When her eyes returned to mine, there was a hint of vulnerability in her gaze. She was open with me, not putting up any walls like she did with other people.

It only made me want her more.

Silence passed, and we just stared at each other. My brown eyes were focused on hers with sharp intensity. Her green ones were a little shy, like she could feel my desire but chose to pretend she didn't.

There was still chemistry here…hot and fiery.

Or maybe it was just my desperate imagination.

I'd give anything in the world, all the money in my bank account and the deed to my house, if I could just kiss her right now, kiss her like she was mine. My palm ached to slide up those gorgeous legs until I felt her perky ass. I wanted to pull her on top of me, feel my cock slide into that wet pussy, and then come deep inside her like I owned her.

I wanted to live in the past.

But Vic's words haunted me. My own conscience did the same. Did I only want this woman because I couldn't have her? If that were the case, I would still be sleeping with other women. I was monogamous with a woman who had no idea how much I wanted her. It was twisted.

Maybe I should tell her.

But where would it go? Even if I wanted a future with her, I had nothing to offer her. I'd be leaving sometime this year, and I had no idea if I would come back...or if I would come back at all. How could I put her through that? How could I hurt someone I cared about? She wasn't just some random woman who meant nothing to me.

She was different.

So different that I was different.

I pulled myself together and made the right decision. "It's getting late, and I have work in the morning..." I lifted myself from the couch and moved to the door, turning my back on her so I wouldn't have to see how sexy she looked on the couch. I had to force myself to leave, not to entertain myself with thoughts of fucking her on that pink bed.

"Yeah...I should get some sleep too." She walked me to the front door.

Torpedo joined her.

I crossed the threshold then turned around to face her. "Thanks for giving me a tour. It's a great house."

"Thanks..."

I stopped and stared at her, but if I kept staring at her, nothing good would happen.

But she stared at me just as much.

I finally turned around.

"Neil?"

Her beautiful voice stilled me, halted me in my tracks because I could never disobey something so lovely. My heart started to race, exactly the way it did before I kissed her. I slowly turned around and looked at her again, just as surprised by her beauty as the first time I saw her.

"Can I hug you?"

It was a simple request, friendly in nature, but to me, it was the sexiest thing she could have asked.

"I haven't hugged you since you've been back. I just thought..." She never finished her sentence.

I came back to her, and my hands slid around her slender waistline. I pulled her into me with an unbreakable force, my arms turning into steel bars of a cage she could never escape. My chin rested on her head, and I closed my eyes, the muscles of my arms aching because they were so tight. The second I felt her in my embrace, I didn't want to let her go. I wanted to scoop her into my arms and carry her to bed. I wanted to be the man between her legs, to chase off anyone else who was interested by giving her my affection every single night.

But I had to settle for this—an innocent embrace.

Her cheek rested against my chest, and she stayed there, her arms around my waist.

I could hold her all night and watch the sun rise the next morning, but the longer I held her, the harder I became. I wasn't ashamed of my attraction to her, but I didn't want to poke her in the stomach for fifteen minutes straight.

My arms dropped and I pulled away. "Goodnight." I didn't look at her again because I knew what would happen if I did. I kept my eyes on the ground and kept walking.

Her gentle voice erupted behind me. "Goodnight..."

STACY WAS ALREADY at the restaurant, texting on her phone frantically while her iced tea sat in front of her.

I fell into the chair across from her. "Where's that asshole?"

"Late." She kept typing on the keyboard. "Very late."

"What's new?"

"He's in court right now, but the judge doesn't want a recess. He wants to push through."

"They can do that?"

"According to Vic, they can do whatever they want." She put the phone down and gave me her attention. "Unless he's lying and screwing his secretary... She is pretty. Ugh, I hate her."

"You have nothing to worry about, Stacy." If only she really understood how hung up my brother was.

"For now. But when I'm fat and pregnant—"

"It won't make a difference." When my brother was committed to something, he was completely in the game. He puts all his poker chips in the pile. "We were working out last week, and a pretty girl made a move. He was a total dick to her and walked away. Honestly, he's too much of an asshole."

She smiled slightly.

"Don't worry about Vic."

"Well...that's good to know. I know Vic would never do anything like that, but he's such a sexy piece of ass, especially when he wears that suit... Oh man. It's hard to let him out of the house without ripping all his clothes off. And when he's trying a case and getting all red in the face." She started to fan herself. "That man is the sexiest guy—"

"Do you have a point to this?"

"Sorry. My point is, I know I have a sexy husband."

"And you made your point very clear." When a waitress walked by, I ordered an iced tea as well, then looked at the menu. "So, it'll just be us? Is Charlotte coming?"

"No, I didn't invite her."

"Oh..." I hid my disappointment and looked at the salads.

"Vic told me what you said about her."

I lifted my gaze, surprised Vic had betrayed my confidence like that. I knew he and Stacy were close, but I didn't think he would share my secrets with her so easily. Now it was only a matter of time before she told Charlotte and everything would be weird.

Stacy stared at me.

I stared back and didn't confirm her comment.

"The only reason he told me is because I told him Charlotte said the same thing."

Within a heartbeat, all my anger was gone. The chemistry I'd felt between us the other night wasn't just my imagination. Maybe she'd wanted me as much as I wanted her. Maybe she'd wanted to invite me to spend the night but had the good judgment not to. "Go on."

"There's not much to say. I just thought since both of you felt the exact same way...it was weird to keep hiding it."

"Does that mean you told her how I feel?"

"Not yet."

If Charlotte felt the same way, I guess I didn't care if she knew.

"I know Vic already talked to you and I said the exact same thing to Charlotte, but you really should stay friends."

"Because?"

"You have nothing to lose, but she has everything to lose."

"I don't know why you assume that. I missed her while I was gone."

"She missed you too. But is there any chance you'd settle down and be with her?"

"You have to be more specific."

She leaned forward with her elbows on the table. "Is there any chance you'd get married and start a family? Is there any chance you'd retire from NASA and stay on the ground indefinitely?"

It didn't matter if I fell deeply in love with Charlotte; I wouldn't give up my work for anything. The plans were set in motion, and I already had a huge mission coming up— one that would probably claim my life. Even if I survived it, I would probably repeat it, which meant I would never be around. "No to both of your questions."

Her eyes filled with disappointment. "Then leave Charlotte alone."

That was the last thing I wanted to do. "No one dates someone with the expectation of getting married. People date because they enjoy spending time together. They screw because the sex is good. Those memories aren't worth having if there's no ring at the end?"

"Not at all."

"That's what it sounds like."

"Anyone can be in a relationship when they have no idea where it's going to go, but a woman like Charlotte can't be in a relationship if she knows it'll never go anywhere. Most women feel that way. It's not rocket science, Neil. Is someone going to risk getting their heart broken unless there's a chance they might get something out of it?"

"I have tons of flings without even thinking about it."

"Because you never feel anything. But women feel something for you, Neil. You're the kind of man every woman would want for a husband."

That was flattering.

"Just let it be, okay?"

"She wants me and I want her. You don't think it's strange not to address it?"

She shrugged. "Kyle put his heart on the line, and she crushed him. The next day, he pretended nothing happened. They've gone out to lunch, ball games, and acted like everything is perfectly fine."

So, Kyle did make his move. "She said no?"

She nodded. "I was hoping she would give it a chance."

That shouldn't thrill me, but it did. She rejected Cameron, then she rejected Kyle. Cameron was a piece of shit, but Kyle seemed like a nice guy even though I personally didn't like him. He was loyal to Charlotte. Plus, he was strong and good-looking. "Did she say why?"

"Said she didn't want to risk their friendship."

That made sense. She said the same thing to me.

"And she didn't want to sleep with him while she still had feelings for you..."

My neck immediately felt warm while my fingertips went numb. She'd turned down a good guy because she wanted to be with me. She didn't sleep with him because she wanted to sleep with me. I was turning down ass left and right, and apparently, she was doing the same. "And you expect me to do nothing? I think it's pretty clear what she wants." If she weren't at work right now, I'd march over to her house and take her to bed right that second.

"That's how she feels, but who knows if that's what she wants. She was the one who said you should just be friends, right?"

"But we're terrible friends. We're much better lovers."

"Neil."

I sighed when she started to snap at me.

"Don't hurt my friend."

"I would never, Stacy."

"To be honest, I wish she would get with Kyle. Kyle loves her. He's loved her even before Cameron fucked everything up. That's a man who wants to give her everything she wants, who would never hurt her. But she won't listen to me."

"If she doesn't like him, she doesn't like him."

"I don't think liking him is the problem. I just think she's too scared to lose him."

"She just said that she has feelings for me."

"But if she didn't, I think she would give Kyle a chance."

It sounded like I was ruining everything for Charlotte, like I was getting in the way of her happiness. "You know I'm not a romantic guy. I'm not even sure how I feel about Charlotte. But when we're together...there's something there. I haven't kept my dick in my pants this long since before puberty... and we aren't even together. I've had offers from beautiful women, but I always go home alone. I want Charlotte...she wants me. You can keep telling me to leave her alone, but one of us is going to cave. If it's not me, it's going to be her. We need to let it happen and deal with the consequences later."

She sighed as she looked at me. "You're going to leave...so she'll have to deal with the consequences."

9

CHARLOTTE

I SAT AT THE KITCHEN TABLE AND LOOKED AT THE PUZZLE pieces scattered across the surface. I only had one small corner put together, but if I put in enough hours, I would finally get some traction. "Maybe I shouldn't have gotten such a hard puzzle..."

Torpedo lay on the hardwood floor, chewing a bone I gave him.

I grabbed my phone and was about to text Kyle to come over when the doorbell rang.

Torpedo dropped his bone and ran to the front door, barking like we were under attack in a warzone.

"Torpedo, chill." I pulled on his collar and yanked him away from the door. I moved to the front and looked through the peephole to see Neil on the other side.

Instantly, butterflies soared in my stomach and my heart turned weak. The breath left my lungs, and I became so nervous I almost didn't answer the door. The longer I waited, the more my nerves got to me, so I pulled the door open so I wouldn't have time to think about how handsome he looked—even through a peephole.

We came face-to-face, and I smiled like everything was normal. "What a nice surprise." He was in jeans and a t-shirt, his arms getting bigger every week because he was hitting the gym so hard. My smile slowly faded when he didn't mirror the sentiment.

"Can we talk?"

"Sure..."

He invited himself inside then faced me in the entryway.

Now I was nervous all over again.

He stared at me for a long time, his pretty eyes shifting back and forth as they looked into mine. He kept his hands in his pockets, and the affection he showed me last time he was here was long gone.

I had no idea what was bothering him.

He continued to watch me, his gaze making my skin pebble. "I've been home for five weeks. After three months on the moon, the first thing I usually want to do is find a beautiful woman to share my bed. But the last five weeks, I've been alone...because I don't want anyone else but you."

Oh my god.

"I assumed I would stop thinking about you after a few weeks during my mission. But I never stopped thinking about you. I know you said you just wanted to be friends because you didn't want to lose me, but I don't think this heat is ever going to die."

My mouth went dry because I imagined kissing those lips again. I suspected this night would end with us naked in my bed...and that was exactly how I wanted it to end. It'd been a dry three months, full of dates that never went anywhere. I compared every man to Neil Crimson...so no one ever compared.

"Stacy told me you rejected Kyle because you still had feelings for me."

Now I felt like a deer in the headlights, felt stupid that he knew how I felt without my even admitting it.

"She only told me because I told Vic I felt the same way. And I'm glad she did...because I wasn't sure how you felt."

I guess I put up a good front.

He stepped closer to me, his fingertips touching my arm then slowly sliding all the way to my cheek. His fingers migrated to my hair and pulled it from my face, getting ready to kiss me. "Is this what you want? Because if you don't, you only have a few seconds to stop me." He moved nearer to me, his face coming close as he prepared to kiss me.

"I think it's a bad idea..."

He flinched, his fingers halting in my strands.

"I think I'm going to get hurt. I think it'll ruin our friendship. But I want to do it anyway."

His fingers slid down my cheek until his thumb brushed over my bottom lip. "I'll be here for a while, but not forever. And when I leave, I'll be gone for a really long time. I can't talk about the details, so don't ask me. But when that day comes, this is over. And it's over for good."

This relationship officially had an expiration date. "How long until that day comes?"

"Probably a year."

The longer we were together, the harder it would be to let him go. It was a terrible idea, to get involved with a man I couldn't keep forever. It would end in heartbreak. It would end in tears. But I couldn't be near this man without wanting him. I couldn't date other men when he was the only man I actually wanted. I could give in now and pay the price later...or I could pay the price now. Either way, I lost.

"Are you okay with that?" he whispered. He came so close to me that it didn't seem like he cared what my answer was. He was going to have me either way, even if he had to take me.

All I could think about was being with this man, getting lost in the comfort of that deep kiss, being so deliriously happy that all the bad things in life disappeared. I'd have to pay the hefty price later—but that was tomorrow's problem. "Yes."

He barely let me finish the word before his lips were on mine. There was a long pause in our embrace, a gentle halt as we absorbed the touch of our mouths. His fingers slowly glided back into my hair so he could cradle my neck and hold me close. When his lips started to move with mine, a deep breath escaped his mouth, a hint of emotion.

I melted at the sound of his desire. I didn't look my best because I didn't expect company tonight. But he kissed me like I was in a short dress, heels, and no panties. My fingers immediately moved under his shirt so I could feel his flat stomach, so I could feel the hard grooves of his strength. Knowing he hadn't been with anyone else but me turned me on, made it seem like he belonged to me. My fingers dug into his skin at the knowledge, claiming him as my hands slowly eased his shirt off his body.

He took it off for me, letting it fall to a random spot on the floor. His lips were on mine again, this time kissing me harder than before. His hand slid down my back then gripped my cheek in my shorts.

I loved it when he grabbed my ass like that.

He guided me down the hallway to my bedroom and pulled my shirt over my head when we got there. My bra was yanked off before he fell to his knees and kissed my tits everywhere. He gripped one with his large hand then sucked my nipple into his mouth. He sucked hard and squeezed my tit like it was a water balloon about to burst.

I pushed my shorts over my ass and let them fall down my legs.

He grabbed the back of my thong then pulled it over my cheeks, dragging it down my legs until it was in a pile on the floor. When he rose to his feet again, he unbuttoned his jeans and yanked them off quickly, too anxious to wait for my small fingers. His boxers came next, revealing an enormous cock that had made me come countless times.

I couldn't stop staring at it.

I was finally going to get laid.

Thank god. I was so horny, I was about to lose my mind.

He guided me to the bed, putting me on my back because he wanted to take me missionary. "I haven't been with anyone..." He didn't pull a condom out of his pocket or dig into my nightstand. His eyes searched my gaze, asking if I was just as clear or if I had the papers to prove it.

It'd been a long three months because none of my dates went well. I hadn't met a guy who made me so hot that my clothes melted onto my bedroom floor. I hadn't even kissed anyone because the spark was absent. "Neither have I."

His deep brown eyes burned into my face with desire, his cock twitching in approval. He maneuvered farther over me, his knees separating my thighs as he started to smother me with his affection. His hard stomach rested against mine, and his arms locked behind my knees as his hips settled into place.

I was so excited, I thought I might explode. My palms glided over his chest before I pulled him close to me, anxious to feel that cock inside me. I'd fantasized about this moment many times, late into the night with my vibrator, and my memory didn't do reality justice. I gripped his ass and pulled him close to me.

He pressed his fingers down on the base of his cock and guided his tip inside me. Once his thick head found my slick entrance, he thrust his hips and pushed into me hard, wanting to get inside me as quickly as possible.

My arms hooked around his shoulders, and I moaned.

He moaned too.

We sank into each other, our bodies wrapping around each other as we were reunited. The sexy moans he made deep in the back of his throat were the most erotic thing I'd ever heard. Hearing a man feel pleasure made me feel beautiful, like there was nowhere he'd rather be than between my legs.

He started to move right away, thrusting deep inside and continuing to moan. "Jesus." He rested his forehead against mine and moaned once more, his cock so hard, it stretched me to maximum capacity.

I grabbed his ass and tugged him inside me, not wanting him to stop. I could already feel the climax on the horizon, feel my toes curl because the pleasure made my nerves sizzle. My hips rocked back into him, and I took his fat cock with the same enthusiasm he gave in return. We panted and moaned, fucking hard and working up a sweat.

His cock thickened noticeably as he prepared to come, his face tinting red and the muscles of his core tightening. He came with a loud grunt, slamming into me harder as he pushed his come deeper and deeper.

Feeling him come inside me made me explode just seconds later. I took his come and squeezed his dick hard, my hips thrusting automatically because my body was in control now. My mind had been overrun.

Even when he finished, he kept going, staying hard despite the load he'd just given me. His hips kept up the same rhythm, and he rolled his pelvis to rub against my clit. His pretty eyes were glued to mine, claiming me as his woman. He pressed his forehead against mine and kept going. "Your panties are going to be soaked with my come tomorrow."

I ENTERED the data into the computer then moved on to the next sample.

Neil was right. I could still feel his come dripping out of me. We didn't go to sleep until three in the morning, and he got at least five loads inside me before we called it a night. Now

I tried not to smile at work, to skip around the lab like the happiest person in the world.

Kyle stood across from me. "Why are you so happy?" His eyes were downcast, watching his hands as he labeled test tubes and slid them into the slots where they belonged. White gloves were on his hands, and his five-o'clock shadow was thick because he'd skipped the shave for a few days.

I told Kyle everything about my life, from my terrible dates to what Torpedo did the night before. It felt strange hiding the truth about Neil, but it felt stranger to blurt it out considering the conversation we had a week ago. Kyle wanted to be with me—and I said no. Telling him I was fucking someone else was insensitive.

So, I lied. "Thinking about Torpedo."

"Yeah? What did he do?"

I quickly thought of a story I could share. "He hid my keys so I couldn't leave."

He chuckled, twisting caps onto the test tubes. "Little shit."

"It was annoying but also sweet. He doesn't want me to go..."

"Don't blame him." He kept working, like he hadn't just given me a compliment.

I knew I had to tell Kyle the truth, because him finding out some other way was worse. But it didn't feel like the right time, when we were both at work, so he couldn't have privacy afterward.

I'd deal with it later.

"Have plans tonight?"

Neil and I hadn't talked much this morning. He left for

work, and I had to take a quick shower so I could get over here. But I assumed I would see him tonight. If he had plans, I would tag along because I wanted to be by his side as much as possible. "Yeah, I'm going out."

Kyle wasn't nosy, so he didn't ask what I was doing—thankfully. "Want to do something tomorrow?"

I wasn't going to stop hanging out with him just because of the awkward conversation we'd had. He was making an effort to keep everything the same, and I should do the same. And I wasn't going to stop seeing him to spare Neil's feelings. I'd made my choice, so there was no reason for him to be jealous. "I've been working on a hard puzzle. You want to help me?"

"Sure. I'll bring some beers. I wonder if Torpedo will hide my keys so I don't leave."

"Keep them in your pocket...because I wouldn't be surprised."

I'D JUST FINISHED PAINTING my toenails when Neil texted me.

I'm coming over.

I picked up the phone and texted back with a grin on my face. *Presumptuous.*

I know.

Now my grin turned wider.

Minutes later, he arrived at my doorstep, looking so dreamy, he didn't seem real. He shut the door behind him, slid one hand into my hair, and kissed me just the way Vic kissed

Stacy. When he pulled away, his eyes were brighter than before, like he'd been looking forward to that kiss all day.

I knew I had.

His hand continued to rest on my hip as he looked at me. "You hungry?"

"You know me, I'm always hungry."

"Perfect. Wanna go out?"

"Like, to a restaurant?" I blurted.

"No, the flea market." He rolled his eyes. "Yes, a restaurant."

"This sounds like a date…"

He cocked his head to the side. "Is that a problem? A man can't take his woman out to eat?"

Ooh…I was his woman. "I just thought we would spend all our time in bed."

"We did that last night. And we can do that after I buy you dinner."

"I'll put out whether you buy me dinner or not."

He smiled. "Good response."

WE WENT to a steakhouse and shared a bottle of wine. He ordered the rib eye, and I got filet mignon. With a side of grilled asparagus and the biggest potato I'd ever seen, it was one of the best meals I'd ever had.

"I'm so bloated that I'm not taking off my clothes now."

He placed a piece of steak in his mouth and chewed it

slowly. The lighting in the restaurant was dim, but his eyes shone bright anyway. He was the hottest guy in the room, the hottest guy in every room, and he looked irresistible when he chewed slowly like that. "Oh, you're taking them off."

"Maybe after I digest it all."

"I'm not picky, so you have nothing to worry about."

"What are you talking about? You only date supermodels."

"Not true. You're the only supermodel I've ever been with."

It was a sweet thing to say, so I felt the blush fill my cheeks. I rolled my eyes anyway, just to play it cool. "Yeah, right..."

"And I've never dated anyone. We just hook up and sometimes watch TV on the couch. But I don't take a woman out."

"Ever?" I asked in surprise.

"I wouldn't say ever, but it's rare." He grabbed his glass and took a drink.

"So this, right here, is super-rare?"

"Unprecedented. And you really are the only supermodel I've ever been with."

"Stop staying that." I kicked him lightly under the table.

"You've got the sexiest legs, perfect tits, soft hair... You've got it all."

I'd never been given a compliment like that in my life. I looked down at my food and brushed off his words, as if this beautiful man hadn't just said I was beautiful too. "You aren't so bad yourself..."

"Well, come on." He leaned back and pointed at himself. He

smiled, telling me he was joking. He leaned forward and drank from his glass again. "I've got a nice ass that pays for all my meals."

I chuckled. "That must be nice."

"I'm sure your ass gets you free drinks all the time."

I shrugged because I never really paid attention. My stomach was already protruding out so much that I set my fork down and left the rest of my food for leftovers. I'd take it to work tomorrow—or give it to Torpedo if he gave me a guilty look when I came home. "Last night, you said you were leaving in a year and you would be gone for a long time..."

The mention of the subject made him tense, becoming visibly uncomfortable like he didn't want to speak about it at all. "And I said I couldn't talk about it."

"At all?"

He shook his head.

"Because you don't want to?"

"Because I'm not allowed to under federal law. I shouldn't have even told you I was leaving at all, so I'd appreciate it if you could keep that information to yourself. I trust that you'll honor the request."

I assumed his departure had something to do with NASA, but if he was returning to the moon for an extended period of time, why did that have to be a secret? He'd been to the moon countless times. What was different about this mission? "Then why did you tell me?"

His eyes moved to his empty plate as he considered his response. Light music played in the background, and the gentle sound of conversations filled the air. It was a nice place, but since it was a Tuesday, it was quiet. "The last thing I want to do is hurt you, so I want to be as up front as I possibly can. I think you deserve that."

"You wanted to prepare me for the end ahead of time?"

He shrugged in response. "I guess."

"Is this the reason you don't want to settle down? Because you know what lies ahead?"

He held my gaze with unblinking eyes, wrestling with the demons that screamed in his head. He withheld as much as information as possible, but he let a few things emerge. "Yes. I don't want to get attached to anyone when I've devoted my life to this. There's simply no room for someone else, for a wife and kids. I want that to be abundantly clear, that this is a relationship that will end. There's nothing that could happen in the next year that will change my mind, that will change my commitment. I know you want to have a husband and a family someday, so if you meet someone you like...I'll bow out."

Talking about the breakup before we even had a chance to be together was depressing. Last night, I was so high that I never wanted to come down. It was the first time I'd felt complete since Cameron left, being with a man who made me believe in trust again. The idea of letting Neil go bummed me out, but at least I knew the ending at the beginning. I could prepare myself to soften the blow.

At least Neil was honest about who he was.

"I have a feeling that's not going to happen."

His appetite seemed to be fulfilled because he pushed the plate forward to rest his elbows on the surface. His hands were together, showing off his chiseled forearms. Even when he wasn't at the apex of his fitness level, he still had a beautiful body. "What about Kyle?"

"What about him?"

"He seems like a good guy..."

"He is... He's perfect." I didn't have a single complaint about him. He was a manly man, but with a sprinkle of sensitivity. He was kind and compassionate, but if someone crossed him, he had no problem getting his hands dirty. He'd always been there for me, through the good and the bad, and even when I rejected him, he stayed my friend. Not too many people could do that.

"That's a strong compliment."

"Well, he is."

"If he's perfect, why don't you want to be with him?"

I hadn't expected Neil to ask me that. "I hope you aren't jealous..."

"No," he said quickly. "Not at all. I'm just asking as your friend. I'm not the type of guy that gets jealous."

"How do you know if you've never been in a relationship?"

He shrugged. "I guess I'm just secure with who I am."

Vic wasn't the jealous type either, but if some guy kept hitting on Stacy, he would explode at some point.

"Kyle seems like a good guy. He's good-looking and has a great job. There's just no chemistry?"

There was definitely chemistry. When we'd slept together, I had no problem climaxing. "No...it's not that."

"Then, what's the problem?"

"Losing Cameron was hard, and I just don't want to lose Kyle too. Whenever people break up, they never stay friends. They disappear from each other's lives until they're nothing but a distant memory."

"So...you don't want to be with him because you like him so much?"

"Uh...I guess, in a way." I'd never given Kyle a serious chance because I was happily married when we met. And when that marriage went to shit, I used him because I was depressed...which was wrong. Since those lonely nights, I'd been working on myself and trying to put my life back together. "I guess I could see something happening with Kyle someday. But when I met you, I felt this spark between us. I don't know how to explain it, but there's something here that I can't deny." Sometimes there was no explanation for your feelings. Sometimes it was just down to hormones and chemicals in your bloodstream. For whatever reason, Neil was the man who made me feel something, made my heart beat super-fast in excitement. It reminded me of when Cameron and I first started seeing each other...and the adrenaline that rushed through my system at the touch of his fingertips.

"Yeah, I know what you mean." His gaze lowered. It seemed like there was a hint of sadness, a flash of regret.

Or maybe I just imagined it.

"Don't let Cameron sabotage your chance at happiness. If you never date anyone you like because you're afraid to lose them, then you'll only date losers, and that defeats the whole purpose of dating. You deserve to be with a good man."

"That's true...but I am dating you." I wanted to stay friends so we could always be in each other's lives. But my desire for Neil outweighed my pragmatism, and that told me I had much stronger feelings for him than I ever would for Kyle. There was no reason for it. It wasn't because Neil was an astronaut. It wasn't because he was smarter or better-looking. It wasn't any reason at all.

He smiled slightly. "And I'm very happy you're seeing me."

"So, I'm the first long-term woman you've ever had."

He nodded slowly. "Yep."

"I feel like I should get a trophy or something."

He chuckled. "Like a trophy of a Slurpee."

I laughed. "That'd be classy."

"It'd be you." He smiled at me from across the table.

When the bill arrived, Neil immediately grabbed it.

"You know, we live in modern times now. We don't have to do the whole guy pays for dinner thing. We can split it like equals, or at least, take turns paying for stuff."

"I've always been old-fashioned." He slipped his card inside and handed it directly to the waiter so I couldn't intervene.

"Old-fashioned? You ride a rocket to the moon. That's the opposite of old-fashioned."

"Then maybe I'm just a nice guy who wants to buy dinner for a beautiful woman."

Like butter, I melted. "Thanks..."

HE SAT across from me at the dining table and looked down at the puzzle pieces. His fingertips rested across his mouth as his eyes considered his next move. When he was focused, he had the sexiest expression on his face, like he was doing calculus in his head.

I should keep working on the puzzle, but his appearance was distracting.

He reached forward and grabbed a couple of pieces before he started to assemble them on the surface. He didn't even start with a corner. It was a three-thousand-piece puzzle of twenty puppies sitting inside a flower container. They were all the same color and the background was uniform in appearance, so it was a difficult puzzle. But he started piecing things together like it wasn't a challenge at all. Soon, he put together a large picture, making the puzzle come to life.

"Wow, I've been working on this for three weeks, and you've done more work in five minutes."

Neil pieced together a couple more then lifted his gaze to meet my look.

"You do a lot of puzzles?" I asked.

"Not since I was a kid."

Sometimes I forgot he was an insanely brilliant man, that my intellect could never compare to his, that he could work out any problem in seconds when it would take everyone else hours. "It seems like you know what you're doing."

He shrugged. "Our navigation system went out once, so I had to navigate based on the stars and the sun."

"What does that have to do with the puzzle?"

He fit another piece into place. "I'm used to finding patterns in nothingness."

"Or you're just a genius."

He had the humility not to agree with me. "You know who I think is a genius?"

My eyes narrowed. "You better not say me. Maybe Torpedo."

He chuckled. "A genius is someone who questions everything they think and tries to learn as much as possible, someone with the humility to change their mind if their previous assumptions were wrong. They adapt, learn, and grow at such an exponential rate that they are constantly evolving into a better version of themselves. That's a genius."

It was a long-winded answer, but I enjoyed every single word. "That's a thoughtful response."

"People assume I'm a genius because of my credentials, but those credentials don't make me intelligent. The attitude I had to acquire them made me a genius. In the air force, I wanted to learn as much as possible. At MIT, all I cared about was getting it right every time I got it wrong. The desire to be better is what got me here. Even now, I'm striving to be better today than I was yesterday."

"Not a bad way to be." I grabbed a few pieces and tried to fit them together, but they weren't a match.

He didn't tease me for it. "You're a genius too, Char."

"Don't throw that word around lightly."

"You are."

"I'm only twenty-eight, and I'm already divorced. I don't sound too bright on paper."

He lifted his gaze to look at me. "You're divorced because your ex was an idiot. Don't judge yourself based on your flaws. Focus on your achievements. You have a degree in chemistry and work in a lab. That's pretty impressive. You own a house with just one income. Also impressive. And not to mention, you drive stick like a pro and you down Slurpees like they are water. You're the most impressive person I've ever met."

The corners of my mouth ached to stretch into a smile because Neil didn't give compliments unless he meant them. He had already had me at this point, could take me however he wanted, so there was no need to impress me with an ego boost. "I'm glad you find my Slurpee-drinking impressive."

"Any man would." He turned back to the puzzle. "You do these often?"

"Here and there...when there're no games on."

"What are your other hobbies?"

"I don't have very many. I like to hike, go bowling, stuff like that. What do you do?"

"Honestly...I don't have a lot of hobbies. I'm usually working all the time. I guess work is my hobby."

"But your job is so vast in scope that it probably does feel that way. If I worked for NASA, it would probably be my biggest hobby too. A lot of people would kill for the honor, even if you were just a janitor."

He chuckled. "I don't know about that. But I definitely enjoy what I do."

"Have you spent time with Hyde since you've been home?"

"We've gotten a few beers together."

"How's Jane?"

"Good. At least, that's what Hyde tells me." He put a few more pieces together before he abandoned the puzzle altogether and kept his focus on me. "He reminds me of Vic. Wasn't always a committed family guy until he met Jane. The change was overnight."

"What was Vic like before he met Stacy?" I'd only known him through Stacy, so his past was a mystery to me. All I knew was he was a distant, brooding playboy who broke hearts, even if they were made of lead.

Neil shrugged off the question. "You know...how all guys are."

"You're trying to protect him. Sweet."

"I can't throw him under the bus. I don't want to change your opinion of him. He adores you, and you obviously adore him."

"I'd adore him no matter what his past entails. All I care about is the man he's been with Stacy—and he's been the best man ever. You can keep his secrets if you want, but I already knew he was a player."

"Player is kind of an understatement."

"You two are a lot alike."

"Yeah, I guess. But we handle women differently. He was the kind of guy who left in the morning before she woke up with no explanation. He was the guy who ghosted a woman after he got what he wanted. He was the guy who wouldn't sleep with a woman unless she brought her friend to bed too."

"Damn...you weren't kidding." Neil was better-looking than his brother, so I imagined he could do the same thing and get away with it. Based on the limited time I'd known him, he had a similar lifestyle. A beauty queen was in the driveway when I dropped him off—and she looked pissed to see me. "How are you different?"

"I'll usually have a short-term fling, a couple of weekends together. But I'm straight with a woman and will tell her I'll never call her again before she comes home with me. Sometimes, they don't like my abrasiveness. But other times, they appreciate it. I'd rather piss them off up front than hurt them later."

"That's thoughtful."

"Are you being sarcastic?"

"No, actually." Neil warned me what would happen with us, that he would leave and our relationship would be over for good. He painted a vivid picture and gave me the option to decide what I wanted. And knowing there was no romance here, just lust mixed with affection, gave me realistic expectations for the future. I protected myself from day one, and I would continue to do so with an iron shield. "You want another beer?"

"No thanks." His elbows were propped on the table, and his joined hands rested against his lips. Now he stared at me and ignored the puzzle that had engaged him just minutes before. "What about you?"

"What about me? Was I a player in my day?"

"Yeah. I'm sure you broke lots of hearts along the way."

I chuckled because it was ridiculous. "No. Cameron was my first."

Both of his eyebrows rose. "He's the only guy you've been with?"

"No...there were guys afterward."

"But that must have been like one or two. No wonder transitioning into single life was so difficult for you. You've never really been single as an adult."

"Honestly, after Cameron broke my heart, I didn't struggle to adjust. All I wanted to do was pretend I was fine even if I wasn't, so I went on dates and lived the single life like I had a lot of experience in it." I drank from my beer.

"How many guys were you with before me?"

"That's a personal question."

"Sorry...I didn't mean to pry." He lowered his hands. "I wasn't asking in a judgmental way. I was just curious because you fascinate me. You could ask me the same question if you wanted to, but I honestly don't know an exact number."

I knew he didn't ask the question in an inappropriate way. We were sleeping together, so it wasn't that out of line. "I'll answer your question if you answer one of mine."

"Alright. This sounds interesting. What do you want to know?"

"I want to know when you knew Vic was in love with Stacy."

"Oh." He grinned. "That's a good story, actually. He's gonna be pissed that I told you."

"We can keep it between us."

"No, you'll definitely tell Stacy. It'll be impossible to keep it from her."

"Then I'll tell her not to tell him."

"I doubt that will happen either."

"Yeah...you're right. But you're going to tell me anyway." I only heard Stacy's perspective on the relationship, but never Vic's. "After Cameron and I broke up, there were three guys. Kyle, some guy named Ted, and another one named Bryce."

Neil tilted his head slightly, his eyes narrowing at what I said. "Kyle? As in, your friend Kyle?"

"Yeah. Now tell me about Vic."

Neil refused to change the subject. "So, you and Kyle have already been in a relationship?"

Maybe mentioning Kyle was a mistake. "No. It was kind of a rebound situation. Cameron and I had just broken up, and I just wanted someone...and Kyle was there. We hooked up a few times, but I was scared it would ruin our friendship, so I walked away."

"That's pretty fucked up to take advantage of you like that," he said coldly.

"It wasn't like that... I came on to him." I'd kissed him in the parking lot after work and asked him to take me home.

"He still should have been the bigger man."

"No offense, but you aren't any different. Every guy I've been with has been a bit of a rebound."

His eyes relaxed slightly, but he seemed hurt by what I said. "I thought you were over Cameron."

"I am, but I've been having physical relationships because I'm just not ready to be intimate with someone...really intimate. Even though Cameron apologized to me, the idea of trusting someone sounds impossible."

His hostility faded. "I hope that doesn't last forever. I promise you, you'll find a man you can trust—and he'll be worthy of that trust."

"You seem confident that a lot of men can be like Vic."

"*All* men can be like Vic. They just need to find their Stacy." He continued to watch me, his broad shoulders so wide and masculine. His eyes were the only soft feature he possessed. "Vic didn't want to change. He wanted to be a powerful lawyer in the courtroom making a shit-ton of money, and then he wanted to pound pussy at night. Wife? Kids? He said he never wanted that. But then it got complicated with Stacy, and he realized he had to give her those things if he wanted to keep her. And then one day...he wanted those things."

It was so romantic. "I answered your question, now tell me the story."

"True. You held up your end of the bargain." He rose out of his seat then pulled the chair closer to me, so we would be within arm's reach. He rested his elbow on the table, close enough that his cologne wrapped around me. "So I was in town at the time and hanging out at his apartment. We had a few beers, watched the game, and he didn't talk about her at all. He had mentioned he was dating her prior to that, but he never gave me any details. I thought she was more than just a fling, but I didn't think she was special."

"Alright...then what happened?"

"He walked back into the kitchen to get a few more beers

from the fridge. His phone lit up with a text message, and that's when I noticed the photo he'd saved to his screen."

"Was it a picture of Stacy?" That wasn't that incriminating.

"Not only was it a picture of Stacy, but it was a picture of her asleep in his bed."

"Aww..."

He nodded slightly. "A guy doesn't have a picture like that on his phone unless he's fallen hard. Vic was the last person I expected to do something like that, so it was a red flag."

"Did you ask him about it?"

"No. I teased him. He was pissed."

"I wonder if Stacy ever knew about that..."

"I highly doubt it. He would never admit that, not even now."

"What's so wrong about it?"

He shrugged. "It's pretty cheesy, and Vic isn't a cheesy guy."

"Technically...he is a cheesy guy."

"And he doesn't want anyone to know that. People say he's the most ruthless lawyer in Houston. People pay big money for him to represent them in their cases. You think people want to know he's got a soft spot?"

"I think it's sexy when a man has a soft spot—especially for his wife."

"Well, she wasn't his wife at the time."

"Whatever. Still sexy."

He nodded slightly. "Yeah, I guess it is kinda sexy." He grabbed my beer and helped himself to a drink.

I propped my chin on my fist as I stared at him, the lights from the lamp overhead the only illumination in the house. The sun had snuck over the horizon, and now it was pitch dark outside. Torpedo rolled over onto his side and kept snoring, dead asleep because our conversation was boring.

Neil held my gaze without blinking, not intimidated by the intimacy. He leaned forward slightly and kept looking at me, like he might throw me on the table and fuck me in the middle of the kitchen.

I was constantly wet around him, so I was ready to go whenever he was.

But he continued to stare at me. "I don't want to share you." His deep voice came out quiet and masculine, sexy without effort. He leaned closer to me, his hand inching for my elbow.

"That sounds a little cheesy," I whispered.

The corner of his mouth rose in a smile. "I guess you make me a little cheesy."

"Well, I don't want to share you either."

"Good." He tugged gently on my elbow, pulling my hand away from my face so he could lean in closer and kiss me, pressing a delicate kiss on my eager lips. "Because I don't want anyone else but you."

10

NEIL

My life was a fantasy.

I lay back on the bed, my head propped on the pillow while my hands gripped her sexy hips. My fingers pressed hard into her skin, my thighs tightening every time I thrust back into her. She rose up and down on my dick with the sexiest gait, rolling her hips and making her tits jiggle.

She rode my dick over and over, taking all of it while biting her bottom lip.

Jesus Christ.

I closed my eyes and felt my balls tighten, feeling the slickest pussy of my life.

Fuck, was this how addicts felt about cocaine?

My sympathies.

"Neil?" Hyde's deep voice shattered my daydream.

"Hmm?" I opened my eyes, coming back to reality as the

conference room filled with the director and a few associates.

"Don't fall asleep on me right now." Hyde kicked me gently under the table. "You'll make me look bad."

I sat up in my chair, unable to adjust my jeans without the guys knowing why. I wasn't asleep at all. I was thinking about the sex I'd had last night. I'd never gotten so much pleasure from a single woman, had never been fucked so slowly but so passionately at the same time. Cameron had that woman in his arms every night, and he wanted someone else?

Now I wondered if he was gay.

The director passed around the folders and got to business. "I think two pilots are essential for this mission. We're thinking of bringing a third even though the craft can only hold six astronauts. What's your opinion on this? If you agree, who do you recommend?"

I already knew I was part of this mission, but I hadn't known Hyde was—until now.

"Am I part of the Vector mission?" Hyde asked bluntly.

The director looked at us over the rim of his glasses. "Would I have asked you here if that weren't the case?"

Hyde turned to me, looking like an excited schoolboy who just found our moms said we could have a sleepover.

I kept a straight face. "I think two pilots will suffice. We should utilize the remaining seats for other astronauts. We need engineers and chemists for this mission."

He nodded. "I trust your judgment, Neil. I'll take it into consideration. In the meantime, the two of you are leaving for DC. The details of the trip are in your folders. You leave in a few days."

HYDE SAT ACROSS FROM ME, cradling his beer toward his chest like it was a newborn child. He stared at the table with a blank stare then took a long drink, his eyes wide open as if he'd seen a ghost. "It's really happening..."

This wasn't news to me. I'd been recruited for the mission over a year ago. But the fact that Hyde was coming with me was news. "I'm glad you'll be up there with me. Peace of mind..."

"Yeah. Anytime we're together, we have better odds. But..."

"What?" I lifted my gaze and looked at him.

"For something of this magnitude, I was hoping you would be here. You know, in case something happens to me, I know you'll be there for Jane and the kids."

I wanted to tell him his fears were unfounded, but they weren't. Anything could happen. We could die at any moment, for a million reasons. "You can pull out. There are a lot of other pilots who will want the position."

"But none as good as me. I'm the best—second to you."

"Doesn't matter. I'll be fine. Stay if you want to stay. You have a family to think about." This was exactly why I refused to be in a relationship. I couldn't leave behind the woman I loved, leave her to take care of our family alone if something untimely happened to me. I couldn't live with that guilt every time I launched. It was easier to be an unencumbered bachelor. I didn't have to worry about anyone but myself.

"I know…but this is big. This will be one of the biggest missions in US history. I can't just pass that up."

"But it'll be dangerous, Hyde. The director was pretty blunt about our odds."

"They said the same thing about other missions."

"And my father died at a launch."

Hyde dropped his gaze.

"Just think about it, Hyde. Really think about it."

"Are you worried about me?"

I was worried about everything. I was the commander of the mission, and it was my duty to make decisions instantly, to keep my crew alive at all costs. This would be more perilous than anything else we'd ever done. "I'm worried about your family. Because if you don't come back, there's a good chance I'm not coming back. None of us are. That means Jane will be alone."

"She's always known that was a possibility on all my missions."

"But this isn't just a trip to the moon… We're going to Mars."

VIC TEXTED ME. *You wanna get a beer?*

I'm going to Charlotte's tonight. I hadn't talked to my brother about my relationship with Charlotte. As far as I knew, she hadn't seen Stacy either.

Look who's pussy-whipped now, bitch.

Fuck off.

You can't put off fucking for twenty minutes?

We did more than screw, but I wouldn't tell him that. I'd been away for most of my adult life and I knew that bothered Vic, so I caved. *Sure. But I know you wouldn't put off fucking your wife for anything.*

Yeah...but have you seen my wife's legs?

———

IT WAS strange to sit across from Vic with the weight my upcoming task on my shoulders. The date had been set, and now we were selecting the remaining astronauts. The next eleven months would be spent planning, planning, and more planning. Even if I were allowed to share this information with my family, I wasn't ready to talk about it.

They would lose their shit.

"How's that big case you're working on?" I asked.

He was in his gray suit and black tie, looking like a powerhouse with that dark hair and deep brown eyes. He was great in the courtroom because he was relentless like a hungry shark, and he could sway a jury easily because of his looks. Women were drawn to him; men wanted to be him. "I won."

"Of course you did. What are you working on now?"

"Haven't decided yet. I have a few cases on the table, but I'm not sure which I'm going to take."

"Must be nice."

He shrugged. "It took a few years to get my career to this level. I've paid my dues."

"I know you did. And I'm proud of you."

He chuckled like I was being sarcastic. "I'm no astronaut."

"I'm not better than you, Vic. You know that." He'd always been intimidated by my success, living in my deep shadow. But he didn't understand that he was far more impressive than I was.

He didn't respond.

"How's the house-hunting going?"

"I've been pretty busy, so Stacy has been in charge of that. She's found a few places she likes."

"Cool. Got any pictures?"

He pulled out his phone and showed me the listing for the first one.

I saw the price tag. "Wow...business is going really well."

He shrugged. "I've got a trophy wife. Got to put her in a trophy house."

Stacy was pretty, but I never saw her that way. It made his devotion sweeter, because his love was deeper than appearances. "True." I scrolled through the pictures and returned the phone. "Very nice."

He took the phone back. "We've got to make a decision soon. Don't want to be getting all the furniture when the baby comes. Need to be ready for that."

"Good point." I'd be around to see the birth of my niece or nephew, but then I'd be gone shortly afterward. It was a depressing thought.

"So...how are things with Charlotte? Must be good because

Stacy hasn't seen her." Accusation was in his eyes as he drank from his glass, as if he didn't approve of this relationship one bit.

"Yeah, it is good."

"So, what is this? Another fling?"

"I don't know what it is. All I know is we're both only seeing each other, and we're having a good time."

"How long do you think this is going to go on?"

"Wow...you really don't like this, do you?" I always assumed my brother would be on my side, but when it came to Charlotte, he was practically my enemy.

"You know I feel about it, Neil."

I didn't know why Vic felt so strongly about her, why he turned into a territorial dog when her name was mentioned. She was wonderful, but she was also a strong woman who didn't need the protection of a man. "What is it about her that makes you like this? You're a notorious asshole except when it comes to Stacy, so why does Charlotte make you so soft?"

He drank from his beer as he stared at me. When he set the glass on the table, there was a loud thud against the surface. "Because she's family to Stacy, so she's family to me. If the situation were reversed, I would behave exactly the same."

"If you were afraid of some woman taking advantage of me?" I grinned because the idea was preposterous. It was impossible to hurt me because I didn't allow anything that close to me.

"Absolutely."

"Well, I'm not trying to take advantage of her."

"She's just got divorced—"

"Like a year ago. Vic, give her more credit. She's not some delicate piece of glass that will shatter if not handled appropriately. She's a strong woman who can take care of herself. She's got an awesome job, just bought a house by herself, drives a stick... Come on." I raised my hands incredulously. "Maybe she was a mess when Cameron first left her, but she's not that person anymore."

After staring at me for a while, he finally gave a nod in agreement. "I just don't want her to fall in love with you and watch you move on to the next supermodel."

"I've been very clear about my intentions."

"Doesn't mean she won't fall in love with you anyway."

"What makes you think I won't fall in love with her?" I countered.

His eyes narrowed slightly, his head tilting to the side. "Is that a possibility, Neil?"

"It's not impossible. Maybe I'm the one who will get hurt."

"If you really felt that way, why would you leave her?"

I couldn't give him the truth, that I would be on the first manned mission to Mars, and I may not come back. And if I did come back, it wouldn't be for years. Even if I fell madly in love with her and changed my mind about marriage and kids, I wouldn't stay. I was committed to this mission—and I couldn't back out. "We still want different things..."

11

CHARLOTTE

"Wow, you're alive." Stacy was already sitting at the table when I walked into the restaurant and fell into the chair across from her. "I was afraid you'd overdosed on cock."

I rolled my eyes. "You can't overdose on cock. Not possible."

"I don't know...depends on the size. I think I've overdosed on Vic's a couple of times." She waggled her eyebrows then looked at the menu.

"Okay...TMI." I glanced at the menu and quickly picked a salad for an early dinner. "So, how's the pregnancy?"

"Oh, hell no, we aren't talking about that." She pushed the menu to the side, telling the waitress we were ready. "I haven't seen you in weeks, so what's going on with you and Commander Neil Crimson?"

"Well...just cock overdoses."

She rolled her eyes. "I mean, what happened? What did he say to you?"

"Said he hadn't been with anyone else but me…and he missed me."

"Wow…that's kinda romantic."

"Now you know why I dropped my pants."

The waitress came over, and since we were in such a hurry to continue our conversation, we barked orders at her until she walked away.

"I told him I hadn't been with anyone either, so we jumped into bed together, and that's what we've been doing ever since."

"So, he's getting a pussy overdose."

"I don't think it's possible for a guy to overdose," I said. "But we don't just hook up. He took me out to dinner, worked on a puzzle with me, we talk… Stuff like that."

"Wow, that's interesting." She pulled her straw to her face and took a drink of her iced tea. "Neil didn't hook up with one of his regulars when he came home, and he actually took you out in public… That's not like him."

"Yeah…"

"I'm gonna go out on a limb here and say he likes you."

"I think that's obvious, Stacy."

"But he *really* likes you. Likes you in a way he's never liked anyone else."

I'd come to the same conclusion. "Yeah. But he's been very clear about our future. He's not gonna change his mind."

She shrugged. "Vic said he wouldn't change his mind. Look at him now."

"Not everyone gets a fairy-tale ending, Stacy."

"I don't believe that. You'll get your happy ending, Char. It may not be Neil, but it'll definitely happen for you."

I heard those words from people often, but I wasn't sure if I believed them.

"I still think you mean something to Neil. And maybe after enough time passes, he'll realize he can't live without you. The question is, would you want to be with an astronaut?"

"I've never had a problem with his career choice. It's sexy."

"And very dangerous."

"Everything is dangerous. You could get hit by a bus when you walk out of here."

"Don't tell me you don't grasp the fact that Neil's profession is exceptionally dangerous. It's the most dangerous profession in the world."

Yes, I did understand. "I support his passion. It's important to him, so no, it doesn't bother me." I knew Stacy and Vic hated it, and that always hurt Neil. But I saw the way his eyes lit up when he talked about his work, the way it meant so much to him. I would always support whatever he loved.

"Then he really shouldn't let you go."

I wouldn't get my hopes up, because if I did, it would only hurt more when he left. "We should just forget about that, Stacy. Neil and I are having a good time. For now, that's good. He said if I meet someone else I like, he'll bow out."

Stacy finally took off the pressure. "How does Kyle feel about it?"

Awkward.

Stacy was about to drink her tea again, but she noticed the look on my face. "You didn't tell him?"

I shook my head.

"Are you going to?"

"Of course. But I didn't want to do it right after he told me how he felt. Seemed insensitive."

"If he finds out from someone else, that will be *really* insensitive."

"I know..."

"In Kyle's defense, he's a man. He took your rejection in stride. He still behaved like your friend the next day. So, he deserves more credit than that. I'm sure when you tell him about Neil, he'll have the exact same response."

"I'm sure he will. Kyle is great..."

"But not great enough, right?" she jabbed.

I knew she wanted me to be with Kyle, but I didn't appreciate her pushing it on me. "I love Kyle and think he's such a great guy. So do you. And because of that reason, he deserves a woman who's head over heels and stupidly in love with him. He deserves a woman who appreciates him every single day. That's not me—so I don't deserve him."

The hostility dropped. "You're right..."

"I know I am."

"I think Kyle is used to being with women who want him forever. But you're the only woman he actually wants... A terrible predicament."

"Even so, it's not right. But I'll tell him about Neil next time I see him."

"Good. Because I feel like I'm lying to him by not telling him."

"I understand."

The waitress brought our salads, and we started to eat. It was a bit awkward between us since we had very different opinions about Kyle. But she was coming around about Neil because she thought he actually cared about me. "So...Neil told me a story about Vic."

"Yeah?" she asked.

"I asked him if he knew when Vic had fallen in love with you, so he told me this story..."

"Girl, spill it." Now she ignored her salad because this was much juicier.

"Neil told me they were watching a game when Vic left to grab a beer. His phone lit up, and that's when Neil saw a picture of you sleeping on his lock screen."

"What?" she shrieked. "Really?"

I nodded.

"Aww...that's sweet."

"He told me Vic was a super asshole before he met you."

"No, he was still a super asshole when we met. But he was so hot that it balanced it out."

"I actually think that makes him more romantic, because he only changed when he found the right woman."

"Yeah." She grinned. "That is pretty sexy, huh?"

"Are you going to tell Vic?"

"Probably not. That way, it's my little secret."

I grabbed my fork and kept eating.

Stacy got lost in her thoughts a bit, eating and thinking about the story I'd just told her. There was a slight smile on her lips, so it was obvious she was still thinking about it.

I gave her some space so she could enjoy it a bit longer. "So, I never told you Cameron stopped by."

"Oh my god, he did? What did he want?"

"First, he apologized...which was nice."

"And then what? He didn't try to get you back, right?"

I nodded. "He did."

She rolled her eyes. "Idiot."

"I told him that would never happen and I didn't think we should be friends either."

"Good. You don't owe him anything."

It didn't matter how much I loved Cameron at one point. Everything we built together was destroyed by his unforgivable betrayal. I wished him all the happiness in the world... just not with me.

"So, you have three guys after you. Kyle, Cameron, and Neil."

"I wouldn't put it like that..."

"But that's what's happening."

"I told Kyle no, and he moved on. I said the same to

Cameron, and he moved on too. So there're not three men actively reaching for my affection."

"Spin it however you want, but you're one hot piece of ass."

"I don't know about that, but thanks for saying it anyway."

I STOPPED by Kyle's place before I went home. He had a house in northern Houston, about fifteen minutes away from where I lived. I pulled up to the house and didn't see any cars in the driveway, so he didn't have any company. His truck was probably in the garage.

I walked to the front door and rang the doorbell.

"Don't be home..." I was dreading this. Even if he had a good reaction, it was still an uncomfortable conversation. If it did bother him, he would have to pretend it didn't. And if he couldn't pretend, then I had to pretend it wasn't a big deal... It was so messy. I wished Kyle had never made his move.

It took a long time for him to answer the door, and when he did, he was shirtless. Black sweatpants hung low on his hips, and his tanned skin seemed flushed with blood, like he'd just been working out but he wasn't quite sweating. "Hey. Everything alright?" He didn't let me inside like he normally did, blocking the door with his size.

"Yeah, I just wanted to talk. Are you busy right now?"

"No. But give me a second." He shut the door.

This was even weirder. I even had a key to his house so I could walk in whenever I wanted, that was how close we were. This behavior was definitely unusual. I wondered if

I'd interrupted something important...or maybe I should have texted him first. He showed up at my doorstep all the time, and I didn't think twice about it.

He opened the door again, but this time, a pretty blonde was there. "I'll see you later." He gave her a quick kiss on the mouth before she walked past me and disappeared from sight. She turned past the garage and walked up the sidewalk.

"Kyle, I didn't mean to interrupt anything—"

"She was about to leave anyway. Come in." He left the door wide open then stepped inside, his muscular back so tight that the muscles shifted under the skin as he moved. His shoulders were broad, and his thick arms were covered in a web of veins. His skin was tanner than usual, like he'd been running outside in the morning before work. "You want a beer?"

I wanted to apologize for intruding like that, but it didn't seem to matter. His date was gone, so it wouldn't make a difference. "Sure."

He grabbed two from the fridge and twisted off the cap for me.

"Thanks."

He walked into the living room then sat down, his stomach still flat because he was so fit. He was in better shape than I remembered, tighter and fitter. His hair was a little shorter, like he'd just gotten it cut, and he'd shaved off his beard. Now he was cleaned up, looking like a whole new man.

I tried not to stare at his naked chest, the way his pecs looked like two slabs of concrete. I turned to the blank TV and drank my beer. "I didn't know you were seeing someone." Maybe I didn't have anything to worry about, that he'd already moved on after our conversation.

"I'm not." He grabbed the remote and turned on the TV. "I met her last weekend."

"Do you like her?"

He shrugged and took another drink. "Which game do you want to watch? Basketball and hockey are both on."

It didn't matter to me. "Basketball."

He turned the channel then watched it like nothing was different between us, like he hadn't just had a beautiful woman in his bed before I rang the doorbell. Everything was normal...like that conversation and kiss never happened. "I can order a pizza if you're hungry."

"No, I'm fine."

He didn't ask me why I was there, as if I didn't need a reason to drop in like this.

I was sitting on the other couch, so I moved to be right beside him.

He leaned back against the cushion and kept looking at the TV. "How's Stacy doing?"

"Good. Pregnancy is going well. She and Vic are still looking for a house."

"Buying a house is so stressful. It's so much work that I'm never moving. I'll die in this place."

I chuckled. "Yeah, it was stressful. But totally worth it."

His eyes watched the player move across the court and make the basket. "You want to play ball with us after work tomorrow? It's gonna be me and a few guys from the surgical floor."

"Yeah, sure."

He took another drink of his beer then set it on the coffee table. "What's new with you?"

Kyle and I didn't have lengthy conversations like Stacy and I did. We talked about sports, politics, and sometimes, we didn't talk at all. He was definitely a much chiller friend than Stacy because he went along with anything. "Um... that's actually what I wanted to talk to you about."

"Alright." He turned his gaze on me, looking at me with those sky-colored eyes.

I didn't want to say it, but the longer I waited, the worse it became. "I just wanted you to know that Neil and I started seeing each other again."

There was no reaction whatsoever. He didn't get angry, bow his head in sadness, or show any outward emotion. He turned his gaze back to the TV, his posture exactly the same as before. "Charlotte, you're free to do whatever you want. I don't care if you want to be with Neil or any other guy. We're friends, so I support everything you do. He seems like a decent guy. I just don't want you to get hurt...but it seems like you don't care about that."

The same sentiment had been echoed by everyone else. "Every relationship ends in heartbreak."

He shook his head slightly. "That's only true when you're with the wrong person. And you know Neil is the wrong person."

12

NEIL

I SHOWERED AFTER THE GYM THEN SAT ON THE COUCH. I'D been there for less than five minutes when my phone vibrated with a text message.

I'm coming over.

I smiled as I read her text. *Presumptuous.*

Got a problem with it?

No, baby.

I went into the kitchen and cooked dinner, grilled chicken with sautéed veggies. I'd just finished when a quiet knock sounded on the door. "Come in." I turned off the stove and scooped the food onto two plates.

She came into the kitchen, wearing a loose sweater and skinny jeans. As time passed, it was getting cooler and cooler, the summer humidity mostly a thing of the past. She sauntered toward me, her eyes glancing at the sizzling dinner I'd just made. "I hope one of those is for me."

"They can both be for you if you want."

She snatched a stalk of asparagus and took a bite. There wasn't a sound, but it seemed like an audible crunch filled the room. "Neil Crimson cooks."

"Sometimes." I pulled the piece out of her fingers and took a bite myself. "And I cook pretty well."

She pulled the veggie out of my hand then rose on her tiptoes to kiss me. "But you kiss better…"

My arm wrapped around her petite waistline, and I pulled her close to me, forgetting the food and getting lost in her warm embrace. I turned her back into the counter and cornered her into place. My hand gripped her thigh, and I pulled her leg over my hip. I pressed her farther into the cabinets, letting her feel my hard-on, feel how she turned me on so quickly.

She moaned into my mouth when I hit the right spot. Her arms circled my neck, and she ground against me, kissing me with those eager lips. Sometimes she gave me her small tongue, letting a hot breath escape in my mouth.

I was shirtless, so all she needed to do was pull down my bottoms to get me naked. She shoved my sweatpants and boxers over my hips until my cock was free. Then she pushed them farther down, getting me naked so she could wrap her fingers around my dick and jerk me off as she kissed me.

Damn.

I wished it was summer so she could come over in just a short dress with no panties underneath. I could slide into that pussy quicker, feel that slickness without having to yank off her jeans.

She turned her head and brought my lips to her neck, telling me exactly what she wanted. She tilted her chin back and let me devour her.

I dragged my tongue up her silky-smooth skin then planted a big kiss on her neck, sucking the skin so hard that I felt like a vampire trying to suck her blood. My fingers unbuttoned the top of her jeans before I pushed them down, letting them sink to her knees. I pushed her panties down next, my fingers sliding over her slit so I could feel that perfect little pussy.

She moaned loudly when I touched her in the right spot.

I grabbed her hips and turned her around, bending her over the counter so I could fuck her from behind.

"What about the food?" she asked, her shirt just inches from the plate.

I leaned over her then pushed everything to the side. "I don't give a shit about the food. I'm gonna eat you instead."

SHE WAS FOLDED UNDERNEATH ME, her tits perfect along with every other curve of her body. Her knees were close to her chest as I pounded her into the mattress. My cock could fuck this pussy forever, but it never went dry. She was always wet for me, whether it was three in the morning or three in the afternoon. Every time I thrust, I went balls deep, fucking this woman in a way I'd never fucked a woman before. Skin-to-skin, chest-to-chest, we were one person. I was about to come again. I could feel my balls tightening toward my body, feel my cock aching for release. Charlotte made up for that lonely three months, and these memories would have to be enough to satisfy me during my long voyage far into space.

She grabbed my ass and pulled me deep inside her, her nails cutting into me. "Come inside me, Neil."

A woman had never said that to me, and it was the sexiest sentence I'd ever heard. Like she'd pressed a button on my cock, I pushed all the way inside her and released, moaning like it'd been years since I'd last fucked her. "Fuck..." I felt my load shoot far inside her pussy, mixing with all the other loads I'd given her that night.

Her fingers slid into my hair, and she pulled me close, kissing me as we both came down from our high.

I couldn't stop fucking her.

I'd never wanted a woman so much in my life.

I rolled off her because my body couldn't go any longer. It'd been hours since we started. I needed food, water, and rest. I lay beside her and closed my eyes for a second, ready to sleep hard that night.

She lay there for a few minutes, still because she probably needed the rest as much as I did. Then she sat up and fixed her messy hair with her fingers. I assumed she was going to the bathroom, but she started to put her clothes on.

"What are you doing?"

"I have to go home."

"Why?"

"I have a baby, in case you forgot."

"Why didn't you bring him?"

"I didn't think I was going to be here so long."

"You should always assume you're going to be here long." I forced myself out of bed and pulled on a shirt.

"What are you doing?"

"Getting dressed."

"Because...?"

I grabbed a bag and shoved a few things inside. "I'm coming with you."

"I can just come back after I pick up Torpedo."

"You'll be too tired to come back, and we both know it. I'm coming with you."

WHEN I WOKE up the next morning, I was still tired from all the fucking.

I opened my eyes and grabbed my phone on the nightstand. It was six in the morning. I didn't have to be up until seven, so I had no idea why my body hummed to life so early.

Once Torpedo knew I was awake, he walked up to the bed then lay right on me, hoping I'd take him outside so he could do his business on the grass.

I felt the air leave my lungs when he sat on me. "Geez, you're heavy."

All the movement must have woken up Charlotte because she propped herself on her elbow and opened her eyes. "You can't give any sign that you're awake. Otherwise, he'll keep pestering you until you get up."

"Then what do you do when you just want to lie in bed?"

"Pretend I'm asleep."

"Well, I'm up, so I'll let him out." The second I got out of bed, Torpedo was on his feet, zooming out of the bedroom and heading to the back door. I opened the French doors and let him into the backyard. I put on a pot of coffee.

Looking sexier than ever, Charlotte walked into the kitchen wearing nothing but my t-shirt.

I brought the mug to my lips for a drink, but my eyes were glued to her.

Her long hair was in messy waves, and her tanned legs were hypnotic. Her calves were so toned they looked sculpted out of her legs, and her slender thighs led to a cute knee. She opened the fridge and grabbed a carton of soy creamer before she helped herself to a mug. She was totally ignorant of the way I was staring at her...as usual.

She poured the coffee into the mug then added her creamer, her eyes downcast.

I could stare at her forever.

"We're both up early. What should we do?" She brought the steaming cup of coffee to her lips and took a drink, looking at me through her thick eyelashes.

"You know what I always want to do."

She chuckled before she took another drink. "I think I'm out of commission for a couple of hours..."

"I didn't think that was possible."

"Just a little sore."

"Sorry...didn't realize I hurt you."

"Oh, you definitely didn't hurt me. I liked every second of it. I just think we're doing it a lot...and you're big and I'm small. Simple physics. But we could talk."

"Talking is good... Fucking is better." I leaned against the counter and held the mug by the handle. "But you're fun to talk to, so that works. What do you want to talk about?"

She shrugged. "Sex?"

I chuckled. "Would you want to go out to breakfast?"

She glanced at the clock on the microwave. "Don't have enough time before work."

"Hmm...got anything good here?"

"Frozen waffles...that are expired."

I chucked. "I'm not a big breakfast-eater anyway."

She ran her fingers through her hair as she opened and closed her sleepy eyes. When she brought the mug to her lips, her mouth opened in the sexiest way. With every passing second, she became more and more awake.

"I do have something to tell you. I'm going to DC for a couple of days."

"Oh, vacation?"

"No," I said with a chuckle. "That's the last place I'd go for a vacation."

"And where would be the first?"

I shrugged. "Hawaii? Seems nice."

"It is nice. You see so many special things in space, but you don't get to see how beautiful our world is... Kinda sad."

I'd always been a workaholic. The day I graduated high school, all I cared about was the next thing on the list. I needed to do everything possible to make my dreams come true. There was no time for trips. "Yeah...it is."

"So why are you going?"

"For work."

"I assumed that. But why?"

It was the same hardship our relationship constantly faced, the secrecy I had to shroud my professional life in. "Another thing I can't discuss..."

She sighed and took a drink of her coffee. "Got it. How long will you be gone?"

"Just a few days."

"So...when are you going to tell everyone about this new mission?"

"When I'm allowed to."

She continued to drink her coffee, looking out the window so she could see her dog in the yard. "Well, I should probably head to the gym since I'm up early. I haven't been going lately because I've been busy." She gave me a knowing look.

"But you still got a workout."

13

CHARLOTTE

BEING IN A RELATIONSHIP WITH NEIL, EVEN IF IT WOULDN'T last forever, was nice. Weeks passed until a full month came and went, and I could honestly say I'd never been so happy. The last year had been spent in turmoil, the depression leaking out of my pores like toxins. I was constantly bleeding out, but there were so many cuts that I couldn't figure out how to sew myself back up.

But now...I actually smiled.

Stacy and I stood at the bar on Friday night, and Kyle joined us. In dark jeans and a black t-shirt, he blended in with the darkness of the bar. When he got to the counter to order a drink, the bartender slid him a beer. "From the blonde at the end."

Kyle turned his attention to the woman and raised his glass in gratitude.

She waved her fingers and smiled.

"She's cute," Stacy said. "Are you gonna go for it?"

Kyle shrugged. "We'll see."

"See what?" Stacy asked. "What's wrong with her?"

"I'd sleep with her," I blurted.

Kyle slowly turned to me, his eyes narrowing in interest. "Now, you have my attention."

"I'm not saying I want to bone her," I argued. "I'm just saying she's very cute."

"All women are cute." Kyle drank from his beer. "If you chase the first tail you see, you'll be running around nonstop. And I usually like to do the chasing instead of having someone chase me."

"But this is an easy lay," Stacy said. "Why waste your energy on a maybe when you can have a definitely?"

Kyle watched people dance in the bar, getting down to the music. "I'm not gonna say because I'll sound like an asshole."

"We already think you're an asshole, so just tell us," I teased.

"Alright." Kyle set his beer down. "I get laid all the time, to be frank. I pick up women at the gym, when I'm running in the park, when I get a beer at a bar. Sex is easy to come by. It's just as convenient as the air I breathe. So, I'd rather work for something once in a while, find a piece of ass that actually impresses me. They say too much of a good thing is a bad thing..."

His response made me realize how important our previous conversation had been. All he usually wanted was sex. But with me, it was the first time he'd wanted something more. Rejecting him had been painful for both of us, but now I suspected it had been more painful for him. "I don't think that makes you sound like an asshole."

"Yeah," Stacy said. "You sound like my husband before he was married."

I wondered if he sounded like Neil too.

A moment later, Vic and Neil walked inside, clearly the two best-looking guys in the bar. Heads turned their way, and they must have been having a good conversation because they were both smiling—which made them even more handsome.

Like always, I felt butterflies glide in my stomach, felt my fingertips go numb. I was excited and nervous at the same time. "The guys are here."

Stacy followed my gaze.

I hadn't thought about Kyle until that moment. He and Neil had never really hung out until this point. Kyle said he was fine with my decision, and he behaved like he was indifferent to my personal life, but I wasn't so sure if he was really okay with it. I suddenly felt insensitive and uncomfortable.

I wondered how Neil felt about him.

The guys didn't even make it halfway before a pair of women stopped them in their tracks and spoke to them.

I turned to Stacy. "No punches tonight."

"I'm not gonna punch anybody," she said as she rolled her eyes. "I knew this would happen when I married him. He's gonna get ass handed to him like he's a frat boy at a waxing salon. Nothing I can do about it. Just have to hope he doesn't get tired of me one day..."

"Never gonna happen," I told her.

Kyle stared at the guys too. "Having a desirable partner will make you appreciate him more, make you do more to keep giving him affection and fucking. Because you don't want to lose him. It's the couples who aren't afraid of losing each other that don't work out."

That was exactly what happened with Cameron. When I couldn't give him what he wanted, he found someone who could.

"That makes sense, actually," Stacy said. "Which is interesting because you've never been in a relationship."

"Just because I've never been in one doesn't mean I don't know how to be in one." He turned back to the bar and grabbed his glass.

I kept staring at Neil. He slid his hands into his pockets as he spoke to the woman talking his ear off. He smiled in return, remaining polite, but he constantly kept inching away, like he was trying to exit the conversation without seeming rude.

Vic stepped away. He must have said something to blow off the woman because she didn't try to talk to him again. His eyes were on his pregnant wife as he came to her, as if no one else in the bar mattered to him at all. His arms slid around her waist, and he pulled her in for a deep kiss.

My eyes went back to Neil. I knew we weren't seeing other people, but we weren't necessarily exclusive either. He told me I could be with someone else if I met a man I liked. That must apply to him too because this was a two-way street. I wasn't his girlfriend. I was a long-term fling. I grasped for a better term but failed to find one.

Vic pulled away from Stacy and turned to me. "Kiss him. That'll get rid of his admirer."

I didn't own Neil, so I didn't feel comfortable doing that. If he wanted to talk to her, he had every right to. I turned around and faced the bar, reaching for the drink I had left there. It was a vodka cranberry, but all I really wanted was the vodka.

Kyle glanced at me then faced forward again.

A minute later, Neil slid his arms around my waist then leaned down to kiss me on the neck. His arms squeezed me tightly, and he blanketed me with affection that felt warm on this fall afternoon.

I closed my eyes in response, falling into the comfort immediately.

"What are you drinking?" He grabbed my glass and took a drink. "Vodka cranberry...heavy on the vodka." He grabbed my hips and forced me to turn around. "I like a woman who knows how to drink."

When I looked into his face, all the tension I felt from before melted away. I couldn't be angry at him for flirting with that woman. I couldn't be anything but appreciative that he was there with me instead of her. "Can I buy you a drink?"

He gave me an incredulous look. "Never. I buy your drinks. That's how this works."

"And you know I'd like to trade off."

"Like I already told you, I'm old-fashioned." He noticed Kyle beside me, so he dropped his smile and extended his hand. "Hey, man. How's it going?"

Kyle acted like the sight of us together meant nothing to him by turning to Neil and taking his hand. "I've been better. The girls are pestering me."

"About what?" Neil asked.

He nodded to the edge of the bar. "Pretty lady bought me a drink, so they think I should fuck her."

"Hmm...I can't refute that logic." Neil didn't look at the woman, instead keeping his eyes on Kyle.

"But if I screw every pretty woman who gives me the eye, I'll never have time to do anything else." He turned back to the bar and grabbed his drink.

"He's got a point." Neil turned back to me. "You've got to be selective. Don't want to go home with the wrong woman."

At that moment, the woman who had been talking to him earlier returned for another chitchat. She had a napkin with a black pen. "I found a pen. Could you sign this for me?"

Neil grabbed the pen and signed the napkin on his flattened palm. "Sure thing. Who should I make it out to?"

"Abigail." With wide eyes full of joy, she watched Neil add a note along with his signature. "Thanks so much doing this. I hate to bothering you, but when I recognized you, I had to ask..."

"You aren't bothering me." He handed the note back to her. "Abigail, this is my girlfriend, Charlotte."

Wow, did he just introduce me as his girlfriend?

I was Neil Crimson's girlfriend.

To me, he was just Neil, but to everyone else...like Abigail... he was so much more.

"So nice to meet you." Abigail shook my hand. "You're so lucky. You get to hear all his stories firsthand." She folded the napkin and placed it in her clutch then walked away. She returned to her friends on the other side of the room and showed them the napkin. All of them seemed just as excited to see the signature.

Neil brushed it off like it wasn't his first time.

"So, I'm your girlfriend, huh?"

Neil turned to me, his eyes making him look so unbelievably handsome. "Is that a problem?"

"No...just wasn't expecting that."

"We're a couple that only sees each other. Doesn't that make you my girlfriend?"

"I don't know...you've never had a girlfriend before."

"No, I haven't." He took a drink from his beer. "But I think I like it."

Winter was almost here, so the nice weather of fall was quickly accelerating into a colder environment. We continued to do our outdoor hobbies as much as possible before the cold temperature really struck the city.

Kyle walked up to the golf ball on the green and readied his putter. He lined up the shot, and after a gentle tap, sank the ball in the hole. "You need to step it up, or I'm going to crush you." He bent over and grabbed the ball from the hole.

"Just remember how many times I've crushed you in the past."

"That was then. This is now." He stepped off to the side so I had a full range of motion.

I placed the putter against the ball, checked the distance with my eyes, and then sank the ball in the hole. "Not so arrogant now, huh?" I retrieved the ball, and we walked back to the golf cart.

"I'm still winning, so yeah, I'm a bit arrogant." He hit the gas, and we drove up the path to the next hole. "So, how are things with Neil?"

I was surprised by the question, even though we'd been together for several months now. Kyle and I had our awkward conversation at the beginning of fall, so it'd been a long time. He'd been with many women since then, and whenever he was around Neil, he didn't behave differently.

When I didn't answer right away, he kept talking. "Char, stop walking on eggshells. If he's the man you want to be with, I don't have a problem with it. The last thing I want is for our friendship to be different. I told you how I felt, you didn't feel the same, life goes on. I've moved on." He said all of this calmly as we drove around the curve in the road and approached the next hole.

"You're right...it has been a couple of months."

He parked the golf cart and grabbed his club from the back. "So how are things with Rocketman?"

I chuckled. "Oh my god, don't call him that."

"I think it's a great nickname. So how are things?"

"Good." It felt like a normal relationship, lots of sleepovers, waffles in the morning, and afternoon walks with my dog. He didn't lose interest and run off with someone else even though his longest fling had only been a couple of weeks. The desire was still rampant in our veins, and our deep conversations had led to a stronger connection. Ever since we'd been together, all the demons I wrestled with disappeared. I didn't think about Cameron anymore, didn't have nightmares about the night he left me. My confidence had returned, and my wounds had healed. That was all because of Neil.

But what would happen when he left? Would I be worse off than I was before?

"That's it?" he asked. "That's all you're giving me?"

"I'm happy," I blurted. "We're having a great time, and he makes me happy." That was the best way to describe what I was feeling. It was laid-back and simple, and he seemed like a loyal and honest man. He understood I'd been hurt so badly in the past that he would never do anything to put me in that kind of pain again. So he was honest with me every single day, which was a nice cushion for my heart.

"Good. That's what a man should do—make his woman happy." There was no haunting warning about the pain I would feel at the end. Kyle was nothing but supportive, and it seemed so genuine that I believed he meant those words.

"What about you?"

"I'm seeing someone."

"Like, you saw them last night and you'll never see them again? Or seeing, *seeing* someone?"

"The second. Her name is Lizzie."

"Say what?" I blurted. "You have a girlfriend?"

"Yeah. I wouldn't call it that, but pretty much."

"Where did you meet her? What is she like?"

"She's a pole dancing instructor at her own studio."

"Whoa…that's so cool."

"She's super-fit." He carried his driver to the tee box and set down his ball. "I think she might be in better shape than me."

"I highly doubt it."

He smiled. "She's cool, mellow. She likes beer, so we have a lot in common."

"Is drinking beer your only hobby?"

"It's my favorite hobby." He lined up the shot then swung his club hard, hitting the ball and driving it far over the fairway. It landed on the green, thirty feet away from the hole.

"Wow, good shot."

He stepped away so I had room to take my own shot. "So, when am I going to meet her?"

"How about tomorrow night? She's been eager to meet you guys."

"Sure. I'm free." I lined up the shot and hit the ball hard. It flew across the fairway then landed several feet behind his, but it was in a better spot to make it into the hole. "Maybe she could give me some pole dancing lessons."

"I'm sure Neil would love that."

"I'm not very graceful. I'd probably just fall on my ass."

"You're sexy no matter what you do, Char. Even at your worst."

14

NEIL

I PULLED THE T-SHIRT OVER MY HEAD, GLANCED AT MY appearance in the mirror, and then walked away. I'd never been the kind of guy who liked to wear collared shirts or anything fancy. My closet was lined with short-sleeved t-shirts and occasionally long sleeves for the cold winters. "So, where are we going for dinner?"

Charlotte wore light-colored jeans with fake holes in the material. A loose-fitting pink sweater was on top, making her look like a piece of cotton candy—curvy and sweet. With her hair in slight curls and pink earrings in her lobes, she looked like an executive for Lisa Frank. "We're going out to that burger joint with Stacy, Vic, Kyle, and his girlfriend."

I turned around, an eyebrow raised. "Kyle has a girlfriend?"

"I know... I was surprised too." A brown leather purse hung over her shoulder, and she rifled through it to grab her phone. She stood near the doorway with her hair pulled over one shoulder, her eyes on the contents of her purse. "But that's the truth. Seems to like her."

I was glad he finally got over Charlotte. She'd turned him down, so he needed to move on with someone else. I'd never been jealous of the guy because Charlotte chose me over him, but I noticed the way he stared at her a little too long sometimes, noticed the way his text messages would pop up on her screen all times of the day. I knew they were just really good friends...but I suspected their friendship was based on longing rather than true camaraderie. "That's great. What's she like?"

"Don't know. Haven't met her. The only thing Kyle told me was she's a pole dancing instructor."

"Wow...she sounds like a keeper."

She chuckled. "I guess she's super-fit and they do stuff together...like hiking and hitting the gym."

"Maybe you should sign up for a class..." I waggled my eyebrows.

"Never in a million years, Neil."

"Why not? There's nothing wrong with it."

"I know that. But you have to have super upper body strength to pull that off. Strippers don't get the credit they deserve. They do the hardest workout in the world, and they look sexy at the same time...pretty impressive."

"Baby, you're strong too." As time passed, I started to call her baby more. It used to be an affectionate nickname I tossed out to lovers once in a while, but now the nickname started to fit her like a second skin. I said it more often than using her actual name.

"Not *that* strong."

"That's why you take the class first. When you're ready, you'll hit the strip clubs as the main star."

She rolled her eyes. "You'd like that, wouldn't you?"

"Ohhhh yeah."

She rolled her eyes again and walked out.

I followed behind her. "Maybe I can watch you guys practice."

"In your dreams, Neil. Actually, not even then."

WE SAT in an enormous booth and ordered a round of beers to start off the night. Charlotte got a couple orders of onions rings to start off for appetizers, but the girls devoured those so fast, Vic and I barely got a few bites.

Kyle walked in minutes later, a blonde on his arm. "Shit, Charlotte ate the appetizers already?"

"Maybe if you were on time, you would have gotten a few," Charlotte teased back.

"I doubt it." Kyle smiled then introduced his girlfriend. "You guys, this is Lizzie." With his arm around her waist, he guided her to the edge of the booth so she could sit down. "Lizzie, this is the crew. That's Vic and his wife Stacy, and that's Charlotte and—"

"Oh my god, you're Neil Crimson." She pointed her finger at me, her eyes wide with recognition. "You didn't tell me you were friends with freakin' Neil Crimson." She turned back to Kyle, her eyes full of accusation.

"Well, I guess I just see him as Neil." Kyle scooted beside her.

Now I would be asked a million questions about my job, and the entire conversation would revolve around that for the evening. But if she wanted to make a good impression on everyone, she should limit the excitement.

Charlotte started talking to her right away, probably to control the conversation and keep it away from me. "When Kyle first mentioned you, he was very proud that you were a pole dancing instructor."

Her shoulders sagged slightly like she was embarrassed we already knew that. "I know...he's a bit obsessed about it."

"Isn't it the best job in the world?" Kyle asked. "I love watching her practice...and what comes after."

"Oh my god, TMI." Lizzie nudged him in the side.

"I'm trying to get Charlotte to take one of your classes," I said. But I had a feeling it wasn't going to happen.

"Why?" Lizzie asked, having no clue about our relationship.

"I'm his girlfriend," Charlotte explained. "Neil is just as obsessed with your career as Kyle is."

"It's the best job ever," Kyle said. "Look how strong she is. Show them your guns, baby."

Now she looked even more embarrassed. "Anyway... What about you guys? I know you work at the lab because Kyle told me that's how you met."

I doubt she knew they'd slept together.

"I'm a lawyer," Vic volunteered. "My wife works in public

administration. But she's quitting soon so we can start our family."

"Oh, that's wonderful," Lizzie said. She turned to me. "And I know what you do...obviously."

You and everyone else.

She kept staring at me. "Didn't you just go on a mission—"

"So, where's your studio?" Charlotte asked, interrupting Lizzie before she could finish the question.

She didn't mind the interruption and rolled with it. "It's actually just a few blocks from here."

Charlotte understood I hated to discuss my work, because my work as an astronaut seemed to be my entire identity to people. They were star-struck and crazed, so they asked me a million questions about that. It got exhausting after a while, which was why I was reluctant to meet new people unless it was a woman I might screw.

"I would totally sign up for a class if I weren't pregnant," Stacy said.

"What does that have to do with anything?" Vic asked. "You can ride a pole. You aren't that far along."

"I'm three months pregnant, Vic," she said, looking him straight in the face. "I'm showing through my clothes."

"So?" he pressed. "It'd be sexy to see you dancing on a pole."

"While I'm pregnant?" she asked incredulously.

"Damn right," Vic said. "I'd stuff wads of cash in your panties, but hopefully you wouldn't have anything on for me to stuff it into."

"Aww, that's sweet," Lizzie said. "True love right there."

"I don't know," I said. "I don't think love has anything to do with it. I think Vic is just hard up for his wife. All lust."

Vic shrugged. "Good point. Not romantic at all."

"I think it's romantic anytime a man wants to fuck his wife," Charlotte said. "And only her." She looked down into her beer and took a drink, like she was remembering the way her old marriage burned up in flames. Her eyes lost their light just a little bit, like the pain still haunted her.

Charlotte was the type of person that didn't deserve to feel an ounce of pain. I wished I could erase her thoughts, make her only think happy things. My arm hooked around her waist, and I leaned in to kiss her, because it was the only weapon in my arsenal that I had. It was the only tool I could use to make her feel better.

She kissed me back, her lips slightly confused by the unexpected affection. But she kissed me anyway...not caring about all the people watching.

———

KYLE AND CHARLOTTE went to the bathroom, because they were always together anywhere they went, so the rest of us stayed at the table. Lizzie was alone without Kyle, so she was visibly a little uncomfortable by the situation.

"You're the only girlfriend Kyle has ever had," Stacy said. "So you must be special."

Vic had had a lot to drink that night, three beers entirely on his own. He held his liquor well, but his eyes seemed to be drooping just a bit. Work was stressful, even if he pretended otherwise. He shook it off most of the time, but now that he'd picked up a big case, his nerves were rattled. "I never thought I'd seen Kyle with someone. But maybe he finally moved on after Charlotte."

I didn't think twice about what he said, because I assumed Kyle had told Lizzie about his past. He probably mentioned he fucked his best friend a year ago, and he might have even mentioned he tried to be with her in the past.

But judging from the shocked look on her face, Lizzie had no idea.

Stacy did her best to smooth things over. "Good one," Stacy said as she forced out a laugh. "Like Kyle could ever have feelings for someone...that guy is stone-cold." She turned back to Lizzie. "We're so excited that Kyle has brought you into our lives. Char and I could always use another girlfriend."

Lizzie nodded and forced a smile, but it was obvious a storm was raging inside her. She was confused, overwhelmed, and probably embarrassed that we all knew something she didn't. I felt bad for her, and Kyle should have mentioned his relationship with Charlotte if he wanted Lizzie for the long haul.

When Lizzie wasn't looking, Stacy gave Vic an annoyed look.

Vic shrugged then drank his beer again.

Charlotte slid into the booth beside me, oblivious to the stare she was getting from Lizzie.

Then Kyle returned to Lizzie's side, his arm moving around her shoulders. "I have an idea. How about you give lessons to both Stacy and Char? I'm sure it'll make the guys happy."

"Thrilled, actually," Vic added.

"Sure," Lizzie said. "And I'm sure it'll help you the most..."

WHEN WE GOT to Charlotte's place, we let Torpedo into the backyard so he could sniff around and do his business. We sat on the couch and turned on the TV, winding down before bed.

She grabbed two glasses of water and put them on the coffee table. "I liked Lizzie. She's pretty, easy-going, successful... She's perfect for Kyle. I'd always imagined him ending up with someone like that. You know, fit like him."

"Yeah, I liked her too." I considered telling her what had happened, but she was clearly happy imagining Kyle with a nice girl. And it would make her feel terrible if she knew she was the reason they hit turbulence. So I kept my mouth shut. "Are you gonna take up her offer for some lessons?"

"You aren't going to let this go, are you?"

"Probably not."

"Even if I did, how would you watch me?"

"At the strip club."

"No way in hell am I stripping in a club." She sat beside me on the couch, cuddling close to my side with her legs over my thighs. "You would want a bunch of guys watching me undress and spin around on a metal pole?"

I shrugged. "In my fantasy, I'm the only guy there."

"Well, we can't rent out a whole place, and I'm not putting a pole in my house."

"Then I'll watch you practice."

"That's not gonna happen either. I'd be terrible."

"Practice makes perfect, right?"

She turned her body toward me so our mouths were close together. "How about I just strip and forget the pole?"

"You have my attention."

She got off the couch then played a slow song with a strong beat from her phone.

I sat up straight and rubbed my hands together. "Wow...this is really happening."

"It's the only way to get you to shut up about this pole dancing bullshit." She rocked her hips from side to side, flipped her hair, and then pulled her pink sweater over her head. Now she was just in her lacy white bra, her fair skin so appetizing. She turned around, shook her ass, and then reached to unclasp the back of her bra.

She was actually pretty good at this stripping thing.

She unfastened it and turned around, letting the material roll down her arms as her perfect tits came on display. When the bra got to her hands, she tossed it at me, letting it land in my lap, right over where my hard dick sat.

My arms rested across the back of the couch, and I imagined fucking her as more clothes fell to the floor. My eyes roamed over her curves and gorgeous skin, appreciating all of her so much. I'd been with beautiful women, all different and unique, but there was no one like Charlotte.

She unbuttoned her jeans and then shook her ass as she got the material over her curves. Slowly they slid down to her thighs before she turned around and bent over all the way to get them off. She did the same with her panties.

Jesus.

I got a perfect view of her sexy little cunt, the precisely shaved area before it led to her asshole between her cheeks. She arched her back as she stood straight up, her perfect body visible from head to toe. Her long hair stretched down her back, stopping at the place where the band of her bra sat across her torso. It was a stunning sight, a woman in all her glory.

And I got to fuck her.

Lucky me.

She turned around and propped her hand on one hip. "How was that?"

I couldn't even spit out a sentence because she left me speechless.

"Silence...that's a good sign." She moved to her to her knees in front of me, scooting between my thighs, buck naked. Her small fingers reached for the waistband of my jeans and unbuttoned the top.

I watched her, feeling a rush of arousal in my veins.

She got the zipper down and yanked on my jeans, grabbing my boxers along the way.

I lifted my hips immediately, letting her slide my bottoms off to my thighs. My cock emerged, covered in pulsing veins with a faint twitch of excitement. My crown was swollen with anticipation, eager to slide into her perfect little slit and feel that wet warmth. Watching her strip down to her bare skin was so sexy, the way she showed so much confidence. She was an innately shy person, but when she was comfortable, she could do so much.

I was so eager to feel her on top of me, I almost grabbed her and pulled her onto my lap.

She separated her knees and slowly lowered her body onto mine, her ass resting on my thighs. Her legs were wide open, so her pussy was directly on top of me. Wet, warm, perfect... fucking perfect. Her nipples lightly pressed against my chest as she came close to me, her hair falling around her face in the sexiest way. She watched me, her plump lips slightly parted in anticipation for my kiss.

"I've seen a lot of beautiful things out there..." My palm brushed over her cheek as my fingers dug into her hair. "I've seen the northern lights while I was on a spacewalk outside the ISS. I've seen Africa in the rainy season, seen the brown grass turn to a beautiful shade of green. I've seen every crater on the moon, seen the dark side of the moon. But you, by far, are the most beautiful thing I've ever seen."

It took her a moment to absorb what I said, to feel my words sink deep inside her chest. Her eyes softened, and her lips parted a little more, like she needed more air for her aching lungs. As my fingers moved toward her mouth, she pressed a kiss to my thumb, her eyes still locked on me.

My cock was hard against her entrance, the length covered in the desire that dripped from her body. Nothing sexier than having a beautiful woman on your lap, feeling her ass cheeks pressed against the muscles of your legs. I'd never said anything romantic in my life to anyone, especially something like that, but the words tumbled out as I looked at her. They were so easy to say, so easy to get out while looking into her beautiful eyes. The only time I blanketed a moment with compliments was to get laid. But with Charlotte, I already was getting laid every night. I said those words just to say them, because that's the way I felt.

My hands went to her ass, and I forced her up so I could guide my crown into her entrance. Slowly, I maneuvered her down so my cock slowly slid inside that perfect pussy. Inch by inch, I was reunited with the place I wanted to be most. She was all woman, all curves, all perfection. Like every other time I had her, I moaned like it'd been weeks rather than hours since we were last together.

She moaned when she felt all of me, felt how hard I was for her. Her arms circled around my shoulders, and she rested her head against mine, her eyes closed as she treasured the way I felt between her legs. Her hips rotated slightly, feeling my cock press up against the walls of her channel.

My hands gripped her cheeks, and I started to guide her up and down, pulling her pussy down my cock then pushing her back up again. Every time I sank inside her, I moaned because it felt so damn good. It was the best pussy I'd ever had, the best woman I'd ever had. She was so small, my fingers could span across her waist completely. She had a petite frame but a woman's chest. She was perfect—so damn perfect.

"Neil..." My name on her lips was even more erotic than her moans. It was so personal, so uncontrollable. She closed her eyes as she felt me enter her over and over, felt how hard I was, like I was about to explode any moment.

"Baby, you don't need pole dancing lessons. You can ride this one just fine."

15

NEIL

I walked through the door after work and found Charlotte in my living room. She was already dressed in one of my t-shirts and sweatpants, ready for a nightcap to avoid the cold. Winter had arrived, and the holidays were around the corner. Christmas was always hard for my mom without my father, even though he'd been gone for thirty years. She never remarried...didn't even go on a date.

If I were ever married and something happened to me, I'd want my wife to move on. Find a good man to look after her, protect her, and make her happy. But my mother just couldn't imagine herself with anyone but him. It was romantic—but depressing at the same time. "You look better in my clothes than I do."

"Well, I have tits." She smiled as she walked toward me. She rose on her tiptoes and gave me a kiss as she welcomed me home. We'd been together for months now, making a routine that we were both used to. When she got off work early, she came to my house and got comfortable. She usually started dinner, so a hot meal was ready before I stepped inside the door. The house was cleaner too because she tidied up, did the dishes, changed the sheets on the bed, and did my laundry along with hers.

It was nice.

I'd never been in a relationship like this before, where we were together so often, we were practically living together. It was a real commitment, a man and wife together as one—along with her dog.

I really liked it.

The other women I'd been with were dull and superficial. All they cared about was not having dressing on their salads, hitting the gym religiously every morning, and keeping their fake tans intact. They didn't take an interest in deep conversations, were never genuine in any aspect of their lives.

Charlotte was different.

"True. Tits make everything better."

After a nice kiss, she pulled away, still looking sexy even though all the clothes were too big for her. "Made pot roast stew for dinner. Is that okay?"

"Okay? It's fucking amazing." I could smell it the second I walked in the door. I kicked off my shoes then stepped into the kitchen, seeing the condensation on the lid of the slow cooker. When I looked out the back window, I saw Torpedo sitting on the porch. Now he had his own chair with his own blanket. "What did you do today?"

"Not much. Kyle and I were supposed to go to the movies after work, but then Lizzie wanted to do something with him..." She opened the lid and took a peek inside to check the tenderness of the meat. Her tone suggested her disappointment about the afternoon.

"You don't like Lizzie?"

"No, it's not that. I just don't understand why all three of us can't go to the movies. I feel like I see Kyle less than I used to, and I never see her. Instead of gaining a friend, I feel like I lost one..."

It'd been a month since that dinner at the burger joint, when Vic stupidly threw Kyle under the bus. I'd assumed things would calm down, but obviously, Lizzie didn't like Charlotte at all after finding out how Kyle felt about her. I couldn't exactly blame her...because how could she ever compete with Charlotte? Charlotte was with me, but maybe that wasn't enough for her. Maybe she was afraid Kyle would always have a thing for Charlotte...which was probably true. "In his defense, that's how relationships are. Once you get serious with someone, you spend all your time with them. Look at us. You're practically living here."

"But I still hang out with Kyle as much as I did before."

"Well...things change." I knew it would hurt Charlotte if she knew the truth, that she may be the reason things were rough in Kyle's relationship. It was the first time he'd had a girlfriend, and it would bum Charlotte out to know she was the cause of friction.

"I guess. When Stacy got with Vic, things didn't change with us."

"It's different."

"I don't see how." She pulled two bowls out of the cabinet then scooped up the servings. It was a delicious stew with tender potatoes and carrots, along with generous portions of meat. It was the perfect meal for a cold day like this.

"This looks delicious."

We sat at the table and looked out the window.

Torpedo was oblivious to my presence. He was content to sit outside on the chair, even if the sun was gone and it was dark. While Charlotte's place was nice, there was something he preferred about my place.

"He looks happy." Charlotte had picked up a fresh loaf of French bread, so I dipped it into the broth before popping it into my mouth.

"Because he loves it here. If he could, he would stay here forever."

"I doubt that. Loves you too much."

"He loves you just as much." She ate her dinner with her hair pulled over one shoulder, looking comfortable in my clean clothes. It seemed like she was my wife, waiting for me to come home so we could talk over dinner. It reminded me of the way Hyde described Jane. She was a stay-at-home mother, so she always had dinner on the table, and the kids were tired out from all the activities they did for the day. "Anything interesting happen at work?"

I was working on the new modules for the missions, testing the software for the systems, and doing everything else to prepare for the trip to Mars. The world had no idea what NASA was about to attempt, and they wouldn't until we were a few months away from launch. I couldn't discuss any of it with her, and it felt weird not sharing every aspect of my life. Hyde told Jane everything, even stuff he wasn't supposed to share, but they were married, so it was different. Despite the incredible risk his profession possessed, she was always supportive. I imagined Charlotte would be the same way, but not everyone else. I knew she kept what limited information she had a secret from Stacy because Stacy would have confronted me if she knew something. At least I knew Charlotte was trustworthy.

When I didn't give an answer, she spoke. "Can't talk about it, huh?"

I looked into my bowl and scooped out a piece of meat. "Not really."

"That's too bad. I'd like to know what you're doing while I'm at work."

"Just practicing various models, different training, stuff like that."

"Why would you need new training if you've already done this before?"

Because I hadn't. "It's just different."

"So, are you working on computers most of the time? Machinery?"

"Both."

"So, if something in my house busted, you could fix it?"

I chuckled. "No, I'm not a contractor. But yeah...I could probably figure it out."

"Then you really are the perfect man."

"I don't know about that..." I was afraid what would happen once I left, how she would feel after we'd become so close. This relationship progressed so quickly because it felt natural. I didn't keep my distance from her because I didn't want to...I loved having her around. I never needed my space because I felt incomplete without her. I'd never felt that way in my life. Normally, I couldn't wait to get rid of a woman once we were done having our fun. I didn't like it when they slept over, but I didn't want to be a dick and kick them out. With Charlotte, my morning always started off right when I saw her next to me. "By the way, thanks for changing the subject when Lizzie started to ask me questions a while ago."

"You mean last month?" she asked.

"Yeah...I appreciate it." I looked at my food and kept eating.

She was quiet for a while. "I know people pester you... Does it annoy you when I ask questions?"

It was so ridiculous, I almost rolled his eyes. "Not at all, baby."

"I guess that makes sense...since I'm sleeping with you."

"It's not just that."

"Because I do other dirty things?" She waggled her eyebrows.

"Well...it doesn't hurt."

She chuckled then kept eating. "How's Hyde? I haven't seen him in a while."

"Good. We see each other at work all the time."

"Wasn't that always the case?"

"No. We're only together now because he's joining me on my next mission."

"Oh, he's coming with you?" she asked in surprise. "That's good news. You'll have a friend along for the ride."

"Yeah. We haven't been seeing each other outside of work because he's been with Jane and the kids a lot."

"Because you'll be gone a long time, right?"

I nodded.

"How long...exactly?" She stared into her bowl, and she scooped her spoon into the potatoes and carrots.

As more time passed, the more difficult it became to keep everything a secret. I trusted Charlotte to keep their information to herself, but I knew the second I told her, our relationship would be different. "A long time... I'll leave it at that."

"Like...six months? A year?"

I knew exactly why she was asking, and I didn't have the heart to tell her the truth. "I can't say... I'm sorry."

She turned her gaze back to her pot roast and didn't ask any more questions. She released a quiet sigh, her disappointment audible.

I felt like a dick for not confiding in her. But I knew if I did, it would be a mistake. "How was your day?"

16

CHARLOTTE

I texted Kyle, and he didn't text me back.

For two days.

When I saw him at work on Monday, he acted like nothing had happened.

"Everything okay?" I stood on the opposite side of the counter from him, checking the labels on the vials to make sure everything was in order.

"Yeah. Why wouldn't it be?" His eyes were on his hands, watching his movements as he used his lab equipment. His white coat was tight on his muscular arms. He seemed to have gotten bigger in the last few months, probably because he did a lot more exercise with Lizzie. She was super-fit, with defined arms and a size zero waistline. Having a super-hot girlfriend like that probably forced him to get into the best shape of his life.

"Because I texted you a couple of days ago and never got a

response." I knew Kyle was busy and forgetful, but he'd never neglected to acknowledge me before.

"Oh yeah. I got sidetracked and forgot." Not once did he look at me. He kept working like this was a casual conversation about our favorite basketball team.

"You've never forgotten before." I didn't mean to cause conflict, but something told me he was lying. Now that he was over me and with someone else, maybe I wasn't a priority to him, but I knew our friendship meant the world to him. He couldn't throw me out just because he'd found a woman he wanted to be with.

"I said, I forgot." He looked up and met my gaze, this time a little hostile.

This didn't feel like the Kyle I knew. This felt like someone completely different, someone I hardly knew. He'd never gotten angry at me, not even when I shot him down. He'd always been a little short, a little quiet, but never outright annoyed like this.

I lowered my gaze and got back to work. "Alright..."

"HE TOTALLY IGNORED me then acted like he hated me. It was the weirdest thing." I sat across from Stacy at the bar. Normally, I felt too guilty to drink since she couldn't, but I ordered a vodka cranberry anyway.

Stacy suffered alone with her iced tea. "Don't get mad at me...but do you think you're just angry because you aren't the center of his universe?"

I gave her an ice-cold stare, offended she would even think

that. "That's so ridiculous. I'm madly in...very happy with Neil." I didn't even realize how deep I was into this until those words tumbled out of my mouth.

Stacy's eyes widened. "Char—"

"I'm not upset that Kyle doesn't have feelings for me anymore. I'm happy he has someone. I just thought Lizzie would be a part of our group. It seems like she's removed him from our lives. And now he's different... Something isn't right."

Stacy's suspicion died away, and she didn't give me shit about what I just said. "Well...at that dinner Vic said something really stupid..."

"What do you mean?" I almost ordered another vodka cranberry, but that would be one too many, so I focused on what Stacy was saying. "Vic always does stupid things. What did he do this time?"

"When all six of us got together for dinner, you and Kyle went to the bathroom. And Vic stupidly mentioned Kyle's feelings for you."

No way. "You're joking..."

"No."

"Why didn't you tell me this two months ago?"

"I assumed it would blow over, and I didn't want to make you feel bad."

I slapped my palms to my face. "I really hope that isn't the reason everything is different. It's been two months, so would that really be a problem?"

"If Kyle her you slept together...it might be. She might see you as the one who got away. Honestly, I can't blame her for being threatened by you. Kyle has been into you for so long, and she knows she can't compete."

"That's stupid. Kyle wouldn't be in a relationship with someone unless she was all he wanted. He's just not like that."

She shrugged. "Maybe Lizzie feels differently."

"And Kyle was mean to me...because she's turning him against me." The idea of losing Kyle terrified me. He was my best friend. He was the guy I did everything with. When Neil left, he would be one of the few people who comforted me. We golfed together, hiked together, did everything together. I really couldn't picture my life without him. "I don't know what to do..."

"I don't think there's anything you can do."

"I could always talk to him about it. I know Kyle cares about our friendship. He might have been annoyed earlier today, but he wouldn't turn his back on me like that."

Stacy shrugged.

"Ugh...why did Vic have to say that?"

She rolled her eyes. "Because he drinks too much. That's why."

"But still...how stupid are you?"

"Kyle probably would have told her you guys slept together at some point."

"But he would have done it more tactfully than that. Can you imagine how she felt? If I were out with Neil and found out he slept with one of his good friends, I'd probably be weird about it too."

"He sleeps with everyone, so that's probably a real possibility."

I didn't see Neil that way at all because he was so good to me. We were together all the time, hardly ever sleeping apart. He was an integral part of my life, like he was my husband or something. That was how it used to be when Cameron and I were together. We were best friends and lovers under one roof. I saw Neil as a one-woman kind of guy.

"Now, back to what you said a few minutes ago..."

I should have known she wouldn't let it go. "I didn't say anything."

"Really?" she asked. "Because it sounded like you were about to say you're in love with Neil. I sincerely hope that's not true, because that would mean you're an idiot who disregarded everything he told you."

"I don't love him." I forced the words out, feeling a pit in my stomach as I made the statement. "I was just making a point. I'm so involved with Neil that I don't care about Kyle's attention. Even if I weren't involved with Neil, I would still feel that way."

Her eyebrow was arched high into the sky.

"I'm serious."

"I don't believe you, Char. And that worries me..."

It was impossible to lie to my best friend. "Well, I don't. I understand my relationship with Neil isn't forever. He's never going to be my husband. He'll only be my boyfriend for a short time...until he's gone."

Stacy didn't take her eyes off me. "I don't believe that...and I know you don't either."

I ARRIVED on Kyle's doorstep and knocked on the door.

It was so quiet it didn't seem like he was home, but his truck was in the driveway.

A minute later, his heavy footsteps echoed in the hallway until he halted at the door. He checked the peephole, saw it was me, and then opened it. He was in just his sweatpants without a shirt, lounging around the house like it was a hundred degrees outside when it was actually winter. With one hand barred on the doorframe, he looked at me, blocking my route to get inside.

Like I'd walk in any way... I clearly wasn't welcome.

He stared me down.

I held his gaze, feeling my anger match his. "What the hell is your problem, Kyle?"

"I don't have a problem. You're the one who showed up on my doorstep. What do you want?"

My eyebrow rose in shock. He'd never spoken to me that way before. "What do I want?" I asked incredulously. "To have a beer? To watch a game? Go to the movies? Those are the things I usually want, so why would they be any different now?"

His arm lowered slightly, but he kept up his hostile gaze.

"So...this is it, then? You get a girlfriend who doesn't like me, and we're done?"

"That's a rash assumption."

"So, you're the one who doesn't like me, then?" I snapped.

He kept up his cold stare.

I couldn't believe this was happening, that our physical relationship from the past was tearing us apart now. "Alright, then... I guess I'll go." I turned around and walked down the sidewalk. "Just for the record..." I turned around to face him again. "If Neil had a problem with you, I'd dump his ass in a heartbeat."

For an instant, his eyes softened, like he couldn't keep up the rage he was forcing himself to feel. There were several seconds before he finally blinked, before his rigid features changed. He seemed like he might say something, but words weren't forthcoming.

I knew my friendship with Kyle was over, that he'd picked his girlfriend over me. And while that hurt so much, I refused to show emotion to him. I turned around and walked back to my truck. Just like the night when Cameron asked for my ring back, I waited until I was around the corner to cry.

WANT ANYTHING FROM THE STORE? Neil's text popped up on my phone.

I was lying in bed, thinking about the last conversation I'd had with Kyle. It was stupid to let it bother me so much. If he were really my friend, he wouldn't let a woman come between us. If things were hostile, he would take steps to smooth them over, to prove to Lizzie we were just friends and nothing more. I didn't expect him to dump her—just find a way for all three of us to be friends.

No. And I think I'm just gonna relax tonight. I'll talk to you tomorrow. I'd never turned down Neil since we got together because I wanted to savor every moment while we still had time together, but now, I just wanted to be alone. I was pissed at Kyle, but it was still heartbreaking to lose him. He was there for me every single day after Cameron dumped me—and not just in my bed.

Neil didn't let it go. He called.

"Shit." I watched the screen light up with his name in all caps. His background picture was of the Milky Way galaxy, so it popped up every time he called. I picked up. "Hey…"

His deep voice was authoritative. "What's wrong?"

"Why do you assume something is wrong just because I want space?"

"Because you never want space."

"Well, things change."

"Can we cut the shit, baby?" he asked, his voice abrasive. "I know you pretty damn well. Something is bothering you, and you're going to tell me what it is."

"Wow…bossy, aren't we?" I shouldn't be a dick to him, not when he was being a good guy by checking on me.

"I'm coming over in fifteen minutes. I suggest you take that time to think about your response before I get there." He hung up on me.

I listened to the line go dead, frustrated by his no-bullshit attitude. But at the same time, I was happy he was coming over...because I was more hurt than I cared to admit.

He arrived fifteen minutes later, carrying a bag of groceries so we could make dinner like we usually did. He helped himself inside and skipped coming to the bedroom door. His movements were audible all the way down the hallway from my bedroom. When his footsteps thudded against the hardwood floor, I knew he was coming this way.

I stayed in bed, wearing just his t-shirt and my panties underneath.

He stepped through the open doorway, spotting Torpedo and me snuggled together.

"There's no room for you."

With his arms crossed over his chest, he approached the bed, looking at the two of us. "Seems that way." He pulled his shirt over his head and revealed his rock-hard body, the physique he worked so hard on. When he'd returned from the moon, he'd lost a lot of muscle strength, but he quickly built it up again with a high protein diet and lots of visits to the gym. He dropped his jeans too, stripping down to his boxers before he got into bed.

There was considerable distance between us because a big-ass dog was in the way.

He eyed Torpedo. "Hey, man. You mind?"

Torpedo didn't move an inch.

"Wow, he's usually excited to see me." He stroked his hand over Torpedo's head then behind his ears.

"He knows I'm sad."

"And why are you sad?" He stopped paying attention to Torpedo then rested his head on a pillow. His brown eyes looked into mine, searching for the answer with his gaze. He was a pretty man, too pretty.

I pulled the sheets farther over my shoulder, but not because I was cold.

"I've never seen you like this. So, you're going to tell me, or I'll make you tell me."

"And how are you going to do that?"

He shrugged. "Withhold sex."

"Well, I'm not in the mood for sex anyway."

"Give it a few days, and you'll go crazy."

"Wow...you like to flatter yourself, don't you?"

He scooted closer to me, as close as he could, considering the large object between us. "Tell me I'm wrong."

I held his gaze without saying a word, knowing I relied on his body as much as I relied on food and water.

He kept up his gaze. "Tell me."

I gave up the fight. "It's Kyle..."

"And what about him?"

"I went to his house to talk, and he wanted nothing to do with me. It's obvious Lizzie hates me, and since she hates me, he wants nothing to do with me. I thought our friendship was stronger than that, so I'm taking it pretty hard..."

"It's complicated. He wants to make it work with her, and it's understandable why she doesn't want him to see you anymore. I'm sure it was an ultimatum."

"But I'm surprised he took it."

"Honestly, any woman he sees will have the same reservations."

"Kyle has slept with a lot of women besides me..."

"But he's never wanted any of them but you. Now, he still sees you on a daily basis, still does everything with you. Can you see that realistically working with any woman?" His eyes shifted back and forth slightly as he looked at me.

"I think a woman should feel more secure than that. Nothing is going to happen with Kyle and me. Maybe he had feelings for me in the past, but he doesn't have them now. If he did, he wouldn't let me go so easily."

"Or maybe that's why he has to let you go..."

I held his gaze.

"Because he's never going to move on from you if he sees you all the time."

"That's not the reason. I know it's not."

He shrugged. "It's complicated. You aren't just some random woman he picked up in a bar. You're a woman he continually has a relationship with, one he goes out of his way to spend time with. Judging from the way Kyle is, I don't think he would really do that for just friendship."

"Are you suggesting our friendship means nothing?" I countered. "That it's all just a ploy to be with me someday?"

"Maybe."

"That's extreme, Neil. And I don't believe it for a second."

Neil continued to lie there, his soulful eyes glued to mine. "What are you going to do?"

"There's nothing I can do... I just have to accept it."

"Alright...is there anything I can do to make you feel better?"

I shook my head.

"How about I make dinner? I picked up some good stuff."

"Like what?"

"Like carne asada tacos and rice."

"Ooh...that does sound good."

He smiled before he got out of bed. "I'll whip them up. Nothing gets you out of a bad mood quicker than food."

17

NEIL

VIC TEXTED ME. *WE NEED TO TALK.*

That didn't sound good. Are you always this dramatic?

Yes. I'm a lawyer. I have to be.

But you're dramatic in an annoying kind of way.

Lawyers are annoying. And you're annoying too.

Just meet me, asshole.

Now I'm looking forward to it even less. Fine. Chill.

After work, I met him at the bar. He was in a gray suit and tie, looking like a powerhouse who would destroy you in the courtroom. I was in jeans and a t-shirt since I'd been working on equipment all day. There was no greater certainty that everything would work on the mission than checking it myself. "Alright, what's the emergency?" I sat across from him, drinking a light beer because I couldn't afford the calories or the carbs.

He stared at me with those menacing eyes, like I'd slept with his wife or something.

"Wow...this should be fun. What did I do now?"

"I need you to break it off with Charlotte. Now."

I was getting really sick of my younger brother bossing me around. He kept sticking his nose where it didn't belong, getting involved in my relationship, when only Charlotte and I should have any say in it. "How about you just mind your own business?"

His eyes narrowed like I hit a button. "This is my business. Charlotte is like a sister to me."

"And I'm your brother, asshole. I'm good to Charlotte. I'm honest and loyal to that woman. I told you I wouldn't hurt her, and I'm keeping my word. You're the one who needs to back off, alright?"

"No. You've already broken your word."

"Excuse me?"

He didn't touch his glass of scotch, which was a good thing since he shouldn't be drinking scotch on a Wednesday afternoon anyway. "Just end it, alright? It's run its course, and now it's over."

"It's not over until we're ready for it to be over."

My brother's body tightened further, like he was about to explode like a volcano. "You need to trust me on this."

"What the hell is that supposed to mean?"

"You're going to hurt her. The longer this goes on, the worse it's gonna be."

"What the hell are you talking about, Vic?" Either he was a drama queen, or he knew something I didn't. "I was just with her last night, and she was upset about Kyle. I was there for her. I'm always there for her."

"But you can't be there for her when you break her heart."

"I'm not gonna break her heart, man."

"That's what you think, but you couldn't be more wrong."

"And you say this, why?"

He bowed his head slightly and sighed, like he was wrestling with inner demons. He argued with himself in silence, debating if he should tell me whatever was going through his mind.

"Vic?"

"I shouldn't tell you this. But I don't think you understand what's right under your nose."

"Tell me what?"

"Stacy was talking to Char, and...Char said she was in love with you."

The words sank into me quickly, like when you had liquor on an empty stomach. It seeped in immediately, absorbing into my bloodstream instantly. I didn't feel anything in response, good or bad. I was just in shock for several seconds.

Vic watched me. "I wasn't supposed to tell you. But since you won't break up with her, you left me no choice."

I reflected on our relationship, all the nights we spent together, all the shared showers we had. We used to go out to dinner, but now we always made dinner at home, like a married couple that wanted their privacy. We were constantly fucking, never getting tired of our time in between the sheets. I knew she cared about me, knew about the affection that burned inside her heart. My brother's announcement was a surprise, but I also wasn't that surprised at the same time.

"It's time to walk away before she gets hurt even more."

That would be the smart thing to do, to leave before our hearts became further intertwined. But the truth was, I didn't want to walk away. I had months before I launched, and I didn't want to spend my last few months alone... wishing I were with Charlotte. "I'm not breaking up with her."

"You fucking asshole." He shook his head slightly. "You're gonna keep screwing her, not caring about the damn mess you'll leave behind?" His voice continued to rise. "You're that selfish? That much of a prick—"

"I'm not going to leave her because I love her too."

Vic's mouth hung wide open because he'd stopped in mid-sentence. His mouth slowly closed as his eyebrows furrowed in surprise. It took him even longer to understand what he'd just heard, longer than it took me to absorb what he'd said initially.

"I love her," I repeated. "I didn't realize it until now...but I do."

OUR CONVERSATION WAS heavy with silence. Vic finished his scotch because his restraint disappeared the second I made my confession. Now he didn't know what to say, how to respond to a declaration like that.

I didn't know what to say either. Those words burst from my mouth before I truly understood the gravity of the statement. Knowing she felt that way about me only encouraged those feelings to rise to the surface. All our nights together, all the drives we took to pick up Slurpees in the dark with her dog in the back seat, told me she was all I wanted.

Vic dragged his palms down his face before they slapped the surface of the table. "So, what does that mean?"

"It doesn't mean anything."

"That's not possible. It changes everything, Neil."

I didn't see why it had to. I wouldn't run home and tell her my deepest feelings. She wouldn't tell me either. It was nice to be together without having to acknowledge it. If either one of us really paid attention, we would know exactly how the other felt. "No, it doesn't."

"If you love this woman, you can't keep launching into space."

"Military personnel deploy and leave their families all the time, Vic."

"That's different. They can still talk on the phone or do video chat. You're not even on this planet."

I loved Charlotte...but my passion for space exploration hadn't died. I was just as committed to my profession as ever before. It was important, the most important thing I would ever do. "I can't walk away, Vic. Charlotte would never want me to anyway."

Vic clearly hoped that this revelation would reverse my commitment to NASA, and when it didn't, he couldn't hide his disappointment. "Then what's your plan? You're going to stay together and leave her here alone? She wants a family, Vic."

Nothing had changed. The agreement we made a long time ago was still intact. "I'll never tell her how I feel because this isn't going to last forever. I understand we want different things, and she deserves someone better than me. So, when the time comes...I'll leave."

"You love her, but you're still going to break up with her?"

"I have to."

"I don't see why."

My mission to Mars could last three years. That was far too long to make Charlotte wait. And there was always a possibility I wouldn't come back at all. "I'm never going to want kids. That's something I'll never change my mind about."

"Why?"

"Because I don't want to be the kind of father who's never around."

"Are you saying dad was a bad father?"

"No. But if he lived, we never would have seen him. Being an astronaut is an ironclad commitment. I don't have time to be distracted by my family on Earth."

"Neil, lots of astronauts have families."

"Yes...and it kills them every time they have to leave. I'm afraid if I have a family, I'll throw in the towel and give up on my dream."

"You've been living the dream for years, Neil. One day, you're going to be too old to do this shit, and you're going to want something else in your life to give it meaning."

"Maybe. Maybe not."

Vic sighed in annoyance. "So, your genius plan is to never tell the woman you love how you really feel, let her go and fall in love with someone else, and then continue to launch into the eternal loneliness of space?"

I didn't appreciate his sarcasm, but I didn't rise to the insult. "You wouldn't understand."

"You're right, Neil." He shook his head. "I don't understand. I don't understand how this could take precedence over living your own life. When was the last time you took a vacation?"

"I've been to the moon, asshole. How many people can say that?"

His eyes narrowed. "I'm gonna have two kids. You'll have two nieces and nephews. You don't want to stick around for them?"

"Of course I do. But I need to do this." I was committed to the mission, and I couldn't pull out. If I returned alive, there was a good chance I would never launch into space again. The physical toll it would take on my body might be irreversible. I might continue to be an engineer for NASA but a retired astronaut. If that happened, I would accept it. But I wouldn't pull out of the race now when I was so close to making history. "We can keep going around for days and days, but it won't change anything. I've made up my mind, Vic." If he was aware of my upcoming fate, he would probably be more understanding of the situation, but without that knowledge, it was a story full of holes.

"I told you not to hurt her."

"I know. But remember, I'm getting hurt too."

He shook his head. "It's different with her. She's already been through so much."

"Heartbreak is shitty, no matter how often or little it happens. If I could take all the heartbreak, I would. Trust me."

Vic stared into his empty glass, his arms resting on the table. "With you out of the picture, Kyle is going to try again. He might succeed this time, and by the time you pull your head out of your ass, it might be too late."

"He's with Lizzie now."

"Come on, we know that's just a rebound."

"I don't know...he stopped being friends with Charlotte because of it."

"But the second Charlotte is available again, he'll dump that woman and chase after her. I don't know what the hell Cameron was thinking, but Charlotte is an exceptional woman. She's pretty, smart, funny, chill... She's a dream woman."

"Trust me, I know she is." She slept beside me every night. She looked at me with those beautiful green eyes and stared straight into my soul. I would miss her every single day when she was gone. Every time I was with someone else, I'd wish I were with her.

"But that's still not enough..."

18

CHARLOTTE

I GOT TO WORK THE NEXT MORNING AND PUT ON MY COAT. MY job could be mediocre and boring sometimes, but I always enjoyed it. My work was important in the system, giving doctors data to treat their patients. There were lots of times when I skipped my break to keep working, even if I didn't actually get paid for it. I wanted people to get the help they needed as soon as possible.

But now, I dreaded going to work.

Because I had to see Kyle.

I'd never imagined things would be this way, that I would picture his face and feel a mixture of anger and disappointment. Now that we weren't friends, we would just stand across from each other and pretend we couldn't see the other.

All because we'd slept together a year ago.

I rejected him because I didn't want to lose him as a friend, but that ended up happening anyway.

I walked to my station, pulled on my blue gloves, and got to work.

Minutes later, he joined me. He stood across from me and picked up his specimens and processed them. Not once did he look at me. He didn't say good morning. Music played over our small music system, but it wasn't enough to cover the silence.

The painful silence.

I sighed as I kept working...miserable.

"WHAT IS IT?" Neil sat beside me on the couch, his fingers running through my hair.

We were watching a movie together, but I'd been zoning out for twenty minutes, thinking about my terrible day at work. Kyle was constantly on my mind. I missed him but hated him at the same time. "What is what?"

"What's bothering you?"

"Why do you assume anything is bothering me?"

"Because I know you."

He really did know me. He somehow always knew when something was bothering me. I turned to him, meeting his gaze as his fingers continued to run through my hair. Torpedo sat on the other side of me, taking up most of the space so Neil and I were pressed together...not that I minded. I looked into his beautiful brown eyes and forgot my troubles for a moment, getting lost in his masculine perfection.

When I didn't answer, he leaned in and gave me a gentle kiss on the mouth. It was a soft embrace, a gentle touch, but it was packed with so much affection, it made me weak in the knees.

I sucked in a deep breath, winded.

He pulled away and rested his forehead against mine, his fingers tucking my hair behind my ear.

He was such a good kisser...damn.

His fingers trailed to my neck as he regarded me, his eyes narrowed. "Is it Kyle?"

"Yeah..."

"Did he say something to you?"

"No...that's the problem. We worked together today, five feet apart, and he didn't say a single word to me. Now it's awkward and uncomfortable. I'm going to have to find a new job because I can't do that forever."

"You shouldn't have to leave. He's the problem, not you."

"I know...but there are other hospitals."

"He's the one who should leave."

I shrugged and kept looking at him, trying not to think about how my friendship fell apart. At least I had Neil...even though that wasn't forever. I would miss his strong jaw, the strong way he grabbed me and held me close. I would miss the closeness, having a man I trusted so deeply. "I'm going to miss you..." Maybe I shouldn't talk about the ending when we still had time together. Maybe I shouldn't admit how much he meant to me. But the words slipped out like I had no control over them.

His eyes softened, filling with sadness and affection. "I'll miss you more."

I highly doubted that, but I didn't challenge him. "I'm done with this movie." I grabbed the remote and turned it off even though we were only halfway through it. I crawled onto his lap and straddled his hips.

His hands immediately moved to my ass, pulling me close to him so our lips were just inches apart. His cock was already hard in his jeans, pressing against me with desire. His hand glided up the back of my shirt so he could unclasp my bra.

My hands cupped his cheeks, and I closed my eyes as I cherished his affection. Time passed so quickly, and before I was ready to accept it, he would be gone forever. I wanted to appreciate every single instant I had with him. And in that moment, my heart ached to tell him how I felt...to tell him I'd somehow fallen in love when I'd promised myself I wouldn't. But I stayed vigilant and kept my secret. "Take me to bed."

He rose to his feet and carried me with no exertion. He kept his face close to mine as he carried me down the hallway and into my bedroom. The hallway was dark, as was the bedroom, ready for us to take off our clothes and enjoy each other. I loved having this strong man on top of me, feeling his sweat slide against my skin as we moved together. I wanted this every night for the rest of my life, and it hurt that it would never happen.

He laid me on the bed then pulled off his clothes, quickly dropping everything until he was buck naked—so damn sexy. With his thick cock and hard body, he was the fantasy I would use with my vibrator. He was a fantasy every woman had, a strong man with a body as beautiful as his soul.

He dragged my hips to the edge and got my bottoms off, letting my ass hang over the edge so he could take me as he stood on his two feet. He left my top on as he gripped both hips and shoved himself hard inside me.

I moaned loudly, clawing at the sheets when I felt that big dick inside me.

He yanked up my bra and shirt so my tits were visible before his hand returned to my hip. Then he kept pounding into me, hitting me hard and deep as he watched me enjoy him.

My hands gripped his wrists, and I held on to him as he held on to me.

"Baby...damn." His core was tight with his exertion, his abs hard as steel and his chest two slabs of concrete. He watched my hips shake as he dragged me to the edge of the bed then slammed his hips into me. Over and over again, we moved.

I never wanted it to end. I used him to drown out my troubles, used him to feel good, to feel beautiful. I used the man I loved...because he was all I ever wanted.

I TEXTED NEIL. *Pizza or pasta?* I was home and standing in my kitchen, unsure if I should whip up some spaghetti or order a greasy pizza. Neil was a lot pickier about his diet than I was, so he would probably choose neither.

I'm gonna be at the center pretty late tonight. Order whatever you want.

You could just go home afterward if you're tired.

I don't care how tired I am. I want to be with you.

My body flushed with warmth, and I imagined myself melting into a huge puddle right on the floor. *Then hurry up.*

Always.

I set the phone down and looked at Torpedo. "He's so dreamy, isn't he?"

He gave a quiet bark.

"I know...I wish he would be your father too."

He barked again then rested his snout on his paws.

"Can't get too attached because he's leaving in a few months...even though I've already gotten attached."

He whined.

"You obviously have too."

I turned back to the TV and finally stopped thinking about Neil when someone knocked on the door. "Hmm...I wonder who that is."

Torpedo hopped off the couch and barked all the way to the front door.

I followed him to the entryway then checked the peephole. "Oh my god, it's Kyle." I spoke under my voice, talking to Torpedo like he was a real person.

Torpedo stopped barking and whined instead. He dragged his paw against the wood, like he was excited to get it open so he could see Kyle.

What was he doing here? At work that morning, it was so tense. Did he come here to scream all the things he was too uncomfortable to say at the time? I'd been hurt by him so much already that I almost didn't open the door because I didn't want to deal with more heartbreak.

But I opened it anyway.

I came face-to-face with him, his hands in his pockets as he wore a long-sleeved olive green shirt. His arms were bigger than they'd ever been, so bulging that they stretched out the material of his shirt. He must have had to buy new clothes because he had to move up his size. Even his chest was bigger.

It had just started to rain, so it fell behind him with the loud splash of drops.

I kept my hand on the door and didn't know what to do. I was frozen in place. This could be a hostile meeting or one of reconciliation. But Kyle didn't apologize for anything, so that didn't seem likely.

After a long stretch of silence, he spoke. "Can I come in?"

Torpedo whined as he walked up to him, standing on his hind legs so he could place his paws on Kyle's stomach.

Kyle rubbed his head without looking at him. "Hey, man."

It seemed overly rude to keep him outside when it was pouring, so I opened the door wider and allowed him inside.

Kyle entered, Torpedo following him.

I shut the door then leaned against it, still defensive. I used to be so relaxed around Kyle, but now I didn't trust him. Without even a slight explanation, he kicked me to the curb and abandoned me just the way Cameron did. But this rejection hurt more...because we were supposed to be friends forever. With my arms crossed over my chest, I asked, "What do you want?" I echoed the same question he asked me when I showed up on his doorstep, being spiteful.

"Alright...I deserved that."

"I'm serious. What do you want, Kyle?" Neil could be home any minute, and I'd rather spend my evening with him instead of fighting with Kyle.

"To apologize. I was a total ass to you...and I'm sorry."

I continued to stare at him, refusing to let my guard down. His apology was sufficient, but I was still in a bad mood. I was still hurt by everything that happened. Some woman came between us so easily.

"You're still mad."

"No. I'm pissed, Kyle. I know Lizzie isn't happy we slept together a long time ago, but you didn't even try to get us to be friends. You could have gotten Lizzie to spend time with me, and she would have understood there's no reason to feel uncomfortable. But you just—"

"She doesn't like you, and she's not going to change her mind about it."

"Wow...that's unfair."

"I told her that."

"I'm with Neil, and you've moved on. Sounds like she's making a big deal out of nothing."

He shrugged.

"I just can't believe you cut me out so easily."

"I didn't cut you out. I was just frustrated by the situation. I have her screaming at me every time you text me, and then I have you still texting me at the worst time. It was a nightmare, and I didn't know how to handle it."

"Well, how are we going to handle it? I'd like to be friends with Lizzie if she would give me a chance. She'll realize she's being ridiculous—"

"I dumped her."

The conversation dropped once he made his announcement.

"She gave me an ultimatum. You or her—I chose you."

I was touched by his decision, but I couldn't bring myself to say it.

Kyle continued to stare.

"What kind of person makes you choose in the first place?"

"A woman who's very insecure around you."

"She has no reason to be."

With unblinking eyes, he stared at me. They were the color of the sky with a tone of hostility. "We both know she does."

"You wouldn't have a girlfriend if you had feelings for me."

"Char, I'm always going to have feelings for you. Sometimes it rises, sometimes it fades, but that overall feeling will always be there. The only way it's going to stop is if we stop seeing each other, or we try to have a relationship and it doesn't work out. When Lizzie pressed me about it, I was honest with her. That's the kind of guy I am...even if it gets me in trouble. So she told me this would only work if I stopped seeing you altogether." He stared at me and waited for me to stay something. "She's not some crazy jealous person. Her concerns are legitimate. And now she knows how I really feel..."

It was an overwhelming amount of information, another dedication of love I didn't know how to process. I didn't realize how serious Kyle's feelings were, that this was an ongoing issue that wouldn't go away. "Kyle...how long have you felt this way?" Now that the conversation was on the table, we needed to address it. I couldn't keep ignoring it and pretending it was a problem that would go away on its own.

He chuckled, even though nothing about this was funny. "Since the day we met."

"What...?"

"Come on, Char. You're smarter than this."

"I don't think I am..."

"Since the moment I laid eyes on you, I've had a thing for you. When Cameron was an idiot and ruined everything, I knew you wouldn't be single long. So I went after you far sooner than I should have. We slept together, and it was obvious you weren't ready to be with anyone else. I backed off and stayed your friend, knowing that's what you needed. Enough time passed and you started to feel better, but then Neil showed up. When you guys broke up, I made another move...but you turned me down."

I felt so stupid. Our entire friendship had been a lie. It only existed because he had feelings for me. "I don't know what to say, Kyle..."

"I don't blame you. It's a lot to take in."

"I guess...I've seen everything with blurred vision."

"Our friendship is real, Charlotte. I've enjoyed the closeness we've had. But I would be lying if I said it didn't make me fall deeper in love with you. You're such an awesome woman. I'd kill to be your man."

Jesus, this was deep.

"But now I realize that's never going to happen..." His eyes drifted down in disappointment. "You turned me down because you were afraid to lose me as a friend. It's ironic."

I felt terrible, felt like a horrible person. I'd been blind to this all along, been so stupid. I was hurting a man I cared about every single day. I kissed Neil right in front of him, assuming his feelings were much less significant than they really were.

"I thought having a relationship would help me get over you, that we really could be just friends. But it didn't seem to help. It just made me hurt Lizzie, when she didn't deserve it. That's an experiment I won't repeat."

I expected an apology and got one, but I also received more than I bargained for. I didn't even know what to say. Kyle had just told me that his feelings had been there even before we were close friends, that he'd always hoped for something more.

Kyle sighed as he watched me. "I'm sorry. I don't know what else to say."

"You don't have to apologize, Kyle. I'm sorry I didn't realize how you felt sooner. I was getting over my divorce, so I wasn't in the right state of mind..."

"You don't need to apologize, Char. Really."

If we stayed friends, Kyle would be in this cycle forever. It'd been over four years since we met, and he was still waiting for his shot. Our friendship wasn't even real because his emotions complicated everything. I knew exactly how it felt to love someone who never loved you back…and I didn't want Kyle to feel that way. I was madly in love with a man who wouldn't stay with me. He warned me he would leave, and he would make good on his word in a couple of months.

I couldn't do that to Kyle. I'd already tortured him enough. "Kyle…we can't be friends anymore."

His eyes narrowed, and his chest halted because he stopped breathing. Everything turned absolutely still once the words were out of my mouth. Confusion mixed with pain, burning in his eyes so brightly, it was like a beacon. "What's that supposed to mean?"

"It means we can't be friends." This was so hard for me to say, to cut someone I loved out of my life. But I wouldn't really love him unless I pushed him away. "You can't keep doing this to yourself. I won't let you. You'll never move on if we're seeing each other every day at work, if we're going to the movies or hitting the batting cages."

"That's a sound argument. But maybe I don't want to move on."

I continued to lean against the door, my arms tight over my chest as my pulse raged in my veins. "What…?"

"I said I don't want to move on." He said the words with more force, making him sound even more confident than before. "You said you didn't want to be with me because you didn't want to risk our friendship. Well, our friendship is on the rocks anyway. Now you've got nothing to lose. You may as well try to be with me and hope for the best."

"Kyle—"

"We'd be great together, and you know it. Neil is just like Cameron. He's gonna leave, and you'll be heartbroken. I can already tell you I'm in this for the long haul, to have babies and all that stuff. I'm offering you something neither one of them did. I love you, Charlotte." He stepped closer to me, his eyes zoned in on my face like he might kiss me.

"Kyle—"

"Give me one good reason why not."

"I'm with Neil."

"He said he would step aside if you found someone you liked. The guy knows this isn't forever. He knows he's not gonna change his mind. Dump him and focus your energy on a man who actually deserves you. I've been here every single day for four years. I've been biding my time, waiting for the perfect woman. Does he see you that way?"

Lowering my gaze was answer enough.

"You're attracted to me. We have everything in common. We have the same career. We want the same things in life. You think I care that you can't have kids? Absolutely not. We'll adopt. As long as I'm with you, I'm happy."

A part of me wished I'd gotten with Kyle instead of Neil. Being in a stable relationship with a man who truly wanted me would be such a nice change of pace. I kept falling for the wrong men, the guys who would never love me. Neil was wonderful...but he would never give me what I wanted. It would only end one way—badly.

"Come on, I know you're thinking about it."

"Kyle...I'm in love with Neil."

His eyes remained steady, but his confidence dipped.

"I don't know how it happened. I told myself not to allow it to happen, but it did anyway. I know Neil is gonna leave me and I know it's going to hurt, but I don't want to walk away any sooner than I have to. Being in love with a man who doesn't love me is painful. It's something I would never wish on someone else...including you. Maybe you're the better choice, maybe you're the guy who can give me everything I want. But Kyle, you're an amazing man. You're handsome, smart, successful...hot. You deserve to be with a woman who loves you the moment she lays eyes on you. You don't deserve to be with a woman who only noticed you because you made her notice you."

"I didn't make you notice me, Charlotte. You've always been attracted to me. Our timing is the problem. If I'd met you before you married that asshole, we'd be happy right now. If I went for you before Neil came into the picture, we'd be happy right now. If we get the timing right, this could be perfect—"

"I just told you I'm in love with someone else."

"But he'll leave you—just like Cameron. And that's when I'll get my shot."

"Kyle...no."

"Yes."

"No. We need to stop seeing each other."

His eyes narrowed farther.

"I can't keep doing this to you, giving you false hope when I have no idea what the future holds. Maybe I'll meet someone else the day after Neil dumps me. Maybe I won't. I can't be friends with someone when there's that kind of pressure. We need to stop seeing each other...for good. I know there's an amazing woman out there for you. Way better than I'll ever be."

"Charlotte, I've been with so many women—"

"I'm not going to change my mind about this. I don't want to see you anymore. I'll move to Memorial Hospital so we don't have to see each other at work—"

"You're overreacting."

"No, I'm not. This hurts me so much, but it's the best thing for you."

"I don't need you to do what's best for me." He moved closer to me, his thick arms stretching his sleeves even more. A shadow was across his jaw, dark like his eyes. He was a gorgeous man, and it didn't surprise me that he picked up any woman he wanted. His body was as beautiful as his face, but not as beautiful as his good heart. "I'm a man who can take care of myself. I don't go home crying like a pussy. I'm patient. And when the time is right, you'll be mine."

That was why I had to walk away, to destroy any shred of hope he had. If I didn't hurt him now, I would just hurt him more later. "I'll never be yours, Kyle. Now get out of my house, or I'll ask Neil to throw you out."

He continued to stare me down like that threat meant nothing to him. "I'm not afraid of Space Boy. I'm not afraid of a man who uses a woman to get what he wants. But I'll leave...because you asked me to."

NEIL LAY beside me in bed, his fingers gently moving up and down my back as he tried to soothe me. When Kyle walked out, I let my tears fall, let my heart sob until my emotions were spent. But my eyes were red and puffy when he came home, so it was obvious I'd been crying.

Now he comforted me...like he always did.

Neil continued to watch me, his eyes full of sympathy. "Now what?"

"I have a lot of sick days I haven't used, so I'll use that time to get into Memorial. They've offered me a job in the past, but I turned them down because I wanted to keep working with Kyle."

"That's a good plan. So, you're never going to talk to him again?"

I shook my head. "I can't keep being friends with him. He'll never move on with someone else if he's always around me... It's the right thing to do."

"You're a good friend. Most women would probably like having a guy under their thumb."

"Maybe...but I love him too much. I only want the best for him."

He pulled my leg over his hip and brought us closer together, our noses almost touching. When he came over, we stripped out of our clothes and snuggled in bed together. Sex wasn't on the table tonight because I just wasn't in the mood.

"Maybe he can still make it work with Lizzie now that you guys aren't seeing each other anymore."

"Yeah..." I didn't tell Neil the entire truth. I told him that

Kyle couldn't move on because we spent so much time together. I kept the rest a secret...since it probably would make Neil uncomfortable. Kyle wanted me to dump Neil since it wouldn't last forever anyway, and I doubted Neil would appreciate it. And I didn't want Neil to know I loved him either.

"Maybe someday he'll fall in love, and then you can really be friends."

"Yeah, I would love that." But even then, I doubted it could happen. If a guy like Kyle had been waiting around for years to be with me, that meant his feelings were pretty serious. And if they were *that* serious, then it would probably always be a problem. I had to accept the terrible truth...that Kyle would never be in my life again.

Neil rested his lips against my forehead and gave me a gentle kiss. His fingertips ran up my back, gently comforting me as I battled the pain inside my chest. He never got angry about Kyle's feelings toward me, probably because this wasn't forever, because I was his girlfriend, but this wasn't a long-term relationship. He didn't get jealous...because I was never really his.

I CALLED in sick for the next few days at work and had an interview with Memorial. Thankfully, I got the job, and they said I could start right away. It was wrong to put my two weeks in even though I took off every single day for sick leave, but it was the only way I could avoid Kyle.

He texted me that afternoon. *I can't believe you're serious about this.*

I blocked his number...even though I felt like shit doing it.

I went to Stacy's place afterward. Vic wasn't home because he was working late on a big case. We sat together at the table, both drinking iced tea because Stacy couldn't have any of the good stuff.

"You got a job at Memorial?" she asked in surprise. "I thought they'd offered you a job with better pay, but you turned it down?"

"I did. But I changed my mind."

"Why?"

The pay was much better. I would be working five days but making three bucks more an hour, which added up to an additional twenty-four bucks a day. In the long run, that would make contributions to my savings and retirement much more sizeable. "Kyle and I...aren't friends anymore."

"Wow, that bitch really sunk her claws into him."

"Actually, he broke it off with her...because of me."

"Oh no. This sounds like a bad story."

"It is." I dug my fingers into my hair even though it made it messy. I didn't care about my appearance anymore, didn't care about anything anymore. "Lizzie wanted him to stop seeing me because she suspected he still had feelings for me. He admitted that he did...and chose me. Then he told me he's been in love with me since we met, and he's been waiting for his chance."

"Wow, he dropped a lot on you."

"Yeah...it was a lot. As he was talking, I realized we can never really be friends. Not now. Not ever. If I'm always going to sabotage every relationship he has, it's just not right. So, I decided to bow out."

"Does that mean you aren't friends anymore?"

I nodded. "I blocked him from my phone and everything."

"Jesus...that's a little cold."

"I have to be. I can't keep hurting him. The less he sees me, the less he thinks about me. Then he'll stop thinking about me altogether...and find someone good for him."

Stacy propped her chin on her knuckles as she considered everything I'd said. "And there's no chance you might want to be with him someday?"

I shrugged. "I don't know. I don't want him to wait around for the slim chance that happens."

"Why is it so slim? When Neil leaves, you'll be alone. Is there really any other guy you'd rather be with than Kyle?"

"I don't know, but I don't want to make a commitment to something when I have no idea how I might feel about it in the future. Maybe I'll meet someone else I like. I don't know. Right now, I'm with Neil...and I'm happy."

"Until he breaks your heart," she reminded me.

Like I'd forgotten how this love story ends. "I know how you feel about me and Kyle. You don't need to remind me."

"I just don't understand why you'd fall for the guy you can't have."

"I haven't fallen for him—"

"I know you're in love with him, Char. Come on, you think I can't tell?"

I lowered my gaze in shame.

"I don't blame you... He's a great guy."

He was more than just great. He was kind, ambitious, amazing in bed... I didn't think I'd fall in love again so quickly. I thought it would be years before my heart was able to feel anything besides heartbreak.

"I just think you need to stop messing around with the wrong guys and start being with the right guy. Kyle is the right guy. I know he is."

"I'm not in love with him, Stacy."

"If you gave it a chance, you would."

"Well, I'm with Neil. I can't even picture myself with anyone else but him."

"I know...but in a couple months, it's going to be over. You'll have to pick up the pieces and start over...again."

And I wasn't looking forward to it. I wasn't looking forward to hitting rock bottom, to watching Neil walk away with a strong back and powerful shoulders. He would move on to the next phase in his life while I remained behind. I would be a memory to him shortly, and when enough women had graced his bed, he might not remember me at all. I'd known this would happen when he came to my door and told me how he felt. I told myself I would deal with the consequences later.

Now, there was no going back. I would have to get my heart broken again...and this time, it would be even worse.

19

NEIL

THERE WAS LITTLE DAYLIGHT LEFT AFTER WORK IN THE winter, so we hurried to the outdoor basketball court to get in a few shots. It was a cold day, but we were dressed in shorts and t-shirts because we worked up a sweat regardless of the temperature.

"Stacy told me about Kyle."

There were times when I didn't like Kyle, the way he stared at Charlotte like she was the only woman in the room...and the planet. I picked up on his infatuation before I even knew how he felt about her. But when I remembered that our relationship wouldn't last, it didn't bother me so much. Kyle was a good guy who cared about Charlotte the way a man should care about his woman. So how could I be mad about it? "She started her new position at Memorial. Seems to like it so far."

"It'll be weird not to see Kyle again."

"I don't see why you and Stacy can't see him."

"I said the same thing. But then Stacy reminded me that the one thing we have in common is Charlotte, so it'll probably be awkward." Vic dribbled the ball then made the shot from half-court.

"I guess you're right."

"It's so shitty, but I think Char did the right thing."

I grabbed the ball and dribbled it a bit before I passed it back to him. "I do too."

"She could leave him dangling forever, but she didn't. That's the kind of person she is, would never hurt anyone if she could avoid it."

He was right. I should have been the same way. I should have stayed away from her so I wouldn't have to hurt her when I left. I could tell her I loved her, but that would just make it worse. It would make her hope for a future instead of moving on to someone who deserved her. I didn't regret the time I spent with her...but I did regret not making a better decision.

Vic dribbled the ball to the hoop then dunked it. "What's on your mind?"

"Just thinking about what you said."

"Seems like it's more than that."

I shrugged. "Maybe I should have stayed away from her. Now she loves me, and I'm going to leave anyway."

He rolled his eyes. "I literally said the exact same thing, Neil."

"I know...but I was too selfish to listen." I dribbled the ball and took the shot. But I missed.

"Too late now." Vic grabbed the ball and dribbled it between his legs. "I hope she and Kyle get together...eventually. He's a good guy who genuinely cares about her. It's unfortunate that you came into the picture and got between them."

"Wow...that's an asshole thing to say."

"Is it?" he asked, still dribbling the ball. "I told you from the beginning I didn't like this. I told you Charlotte needed a good guy, not another Cameron. Don't expect me to take back what I said. I meant it."

"I told you I loved her."

"But you don't love her enough." He jumped in the air and made the shot. "When a man loves a woman, he'll do anything for her. He'll make any sacrifice to keep her. You've made it very clear that your career will always be number one. So, under my definition of love, you don't make the cut." He passed the ball to me, thrusting it hard. "I get that you are a part of something big and special. But love is bigger than everything. If you really loved Charlotte, you would know."

"Ouch." He doubted my feelings based on my actions, but he didn't understand what was on the line. I represented the American people, the population of the entire world. When I'd dedicated my life to this, I knew there would be no going back. I worked too hard to get there, and I wasn't going to step back to prove anything. "When I said I loved her, I meant it. Just because I'm committed to something doesn't negate what I said."

"Maybe. But I also think if you really loved her, you wouldn't let some guy take your spot. You know Kyle will move in once you're gone."

I knew he would take my place instantly, be grateful for the chance to have a woman like Charlotte. Thinking about it made me sick to my stomach. But the idea of asking her to wait for me until I returned to Earth seemed worse. How could I ask someone to wait three years for me? To put everything on hold when I may not come back at all? And what if that wasn't the only mission? What if I took another? That was no life for Charlotte. She wanted the life we had now, where I came home every night and took Torpedo for a walk.

Vic grabbed the ball again and tucked it into my side. He watched me, like he expected me to fire back after what he said. "Right?"

I knew my brother would be over the moon if I stopped everything to be with Charlotte, not just because I would make her happy, but because I would be around for the foreseeable future. But I couldn't give up that dream, not for her or anyone else.

When I said nothing, he dribbled the ball back to the hoop and dropped the conversation entirely.

Because there was nothing left to say.

IT'D BEEN a couple of weeks since Charlotte ended her friendship with Kyle. She was down for a while, but once enough time had passed and the dust settled, she started to return to her bubbly self.

"Every time it's someone's birthday, they have a cake in the break room. It sounds nice in theory, but I keep eating a slice every couple of days. At this rate, this new job will make me gain a couple pounds."

"The more curves, the better."

"Thanks, but I don't know about that." She sat across from me at the dinner table, eating her chicken on a bed of noodles. She was a decent cook when she used her own recipes, and a lot of the time, she had dinner prepared when I came home.

It was nice, because I could imagine how our lives would be if I stayed.

She stirred her noodles around then lifted her gaze to look at me. "You're quiet tonight."

"I'm always quiet."

"More than usual."

I shrugged. "I keep thinking about my last conversation with Vic."

"That doesn't sound good."

"He wants me to stay. He's given me this pep talk so many times, but he doesn't stop. He always has hope that I might change my mind, and when I don't, he's disappointed all over again."

"He just loves you, Neil. Of course, he'll do whatever it takes to get you to stay."

"I know... I just wish he understood."

"Maybe you should take him to the NASA center and show him everything you've been working on. I know he's proud of you. I think he would be prouder if he could be reminded of everything you're doing."

"Maybe. What do you think?"

"What do I think about what?" she asked, her voice growing soft.

"Do you ever think I should stay?"

She stirred her noodles again, like she was stalling until she found the right words to say. She would never tell me she loved me, but would she say the same thing Vic had said to me. When she gathered her thoughts, she lifted her chin and met my look. "I'm kinda biased, Neil."

"Which is why I'm interested in your answer."

She set down her fork altogether, the air growing still as the silence stretched forever. "I think you've worked so hard to get where you are that it would be a waste to walk away now. You're still so young, with so much to contribute. There are so few people with the training and intelligence to do this sort of thing. We need people like you. And even if you never have a family of your own, your work will be your legacy. Your name will always be remembered. It's your passion, what you love, so you should keep going. If you let someone convince you to stay...you'll regret it the rest of your life."

It meant the world to me that she said that, that she understood me so well. She could have tried to convince me to stay, to stay with her to make her happy, but she didn't. She did the right thing...just as she did for Kyle.

"I'll say something to Vic for you."

"You don't have to do that."

"I wish he and Stacy understood everything you do, that they should respect your wishes and be proud of you. I know they love you and want you around, but guilting someone into staying isn't the right way to go about it."

"I don't think anyone could say anything to make Vic see things differently, so don't worry about it."

She turned back to her food and spun the noodles around her fork. "How was your day?"

"Good. Hyde and I are working together on a project. Now we talk all the time...more than I'd like."

She chuckled. "Liar."

I shrugged. "He's my favorite colleague to work with. When we launch in a couple of months, I'll feel better knowing he's with me. He's a good pilot."

"But you're better, right?"

"No such thing as better. You can either fly the damn thing, or you can't."

"Are you the commander of the operation?"

"Why would you ask that?" I countered.

"You were the commander of every mission you've been on in the past."

"Except my first." I was a rookie at the time, learning the ropes.

"I would assume you're the commander this time around too."

"Yeah...I am."

"So...when can you start talking about this mysterious mission?"

"Not for a few months. But when I can, you'll be the first to know."

"Does Jane know?" She took small bites of her food, giving me most of her attention.

"Yeah. But that's different since they're married."

"So, that's allowed? To discuss with your spouse?"

"Not technically. But people need to make arrangements in case they don't come back."

Her skin lightened noticeably at my words. She stiffened, visibly uncomfortable. "That's not going to happen though, right? You're going to come back."

I wanted to lie to her and say whatever she wanted to hear. I wanted to promise her that everything would be okay, that she didn't need to worry about me. But the lie would only hurt more if I didn't come home. This was the most dangerous mission I'd ever been on. The odds weren't good. "You never know what might happen. You could get in a car accident tomorrow and be in a coma for the rest of your life. Everything is dangerous."

"But this is really dangerous, isn't it?"

I looked down at my food.

She took a deep breath then picked up her fork again. "Just be safe, Neil…please."

CHRISTMAS CAME AND WENT, and once the new year came around, everything started to happen so fast. This mission had felt like it was so far into the future, but now it was only a few months away. We were on schedule to launch, and that made the date even more ominous.

I treasured Charlotte even more, like a man about to be shipped off to war. My time with her was growing more limited, but my feelings were also growing. When I was on top of her, my thighs separating hers, all I could think about was the woman underneath me, her bright green eyes as they shone with pleasure. Her fingertips shook as she felt me, the excitement circulating through her like this was our first time, not our hundredth. Her pink duvet cover slid to the floor as we bounced on the mattress, and Torpedo disappeared to the living room to escape our loud noises.

I wanted to be inside her forever. I wanted to stay right there and never leave.

Her palms glided up my chest, and her fingernails dug into me lightly. Her moans filled my ears, made my cock just a little harder every time I heard it. Her cunt was a waterfall of arousal. This woman always wanted me, anytime and anywhere.

I'd been never with a woman more beautiful, more sexy. She didn't even need to try to capture my attention. She always had it, from the way she laughed to the way she smiled. She could ask me to get her a pint of ice cream in the middle of the night, and I would. I wouldn't even blink an eye over it.

I fucked her into an orgasm, pleasure that made her hips buck uncontrollably. Her nails turned into claws, and she left faint marks across my skin, another set to add to the collection that was already there.

Anytime she climaxed, I wanted to do the same. Watching her enjoy me, listening to her moans echo across the ceiling, made me want to follow her into that bliss. I wanted to keep going, to make this session as long as she wanted it to be, but I was too selfish...and she was too sexy.

I came inside her, filling her cunt with another load. All my other senses shut down as I focused on the overwhelming pleasure in my veins. It made all my thoughts seize, made my entire body tense and relax at the same time.

I buried my face in her neck and lay beside her, my arm still holding her because I didn't want to let her go. I felt like I was a million degrees and I was covered in sweat, but I never wanted to lose her touch. I closed my eyes and experienced the high that came after the climax, the peace I felt just being with her.

Then her phone vibrated on the nightstand.

I kissed her shoulder. "Don't look at it."

"Last time I did that, Stacy almost called the cops."

"Let her. I don't care."

She kissed me on the cheek before she grabbed her phone. "Oh my god."

"What?" I sat up. "Everything okay?"

"Yeah...Stacy and Vic just bought a house."

"Wow, that's great." They'd been looking for a long time, and now they finally seemed to settle on a home where they would raise their kids. Stacy was six months along, so they were running out of time. They still had to set up the baby's room and get all of their supplies ready.

"She wants me to ask you if you'll help them move."

"Does she know I'm here?"

"Just assumed."

I chuckled. "Yeah, sure. When?"

"Tomorrow."

"Tomorrow?" I asked incredulously. "They aren't messing around, are they?"

"I know Stacy hates that apartment. There's only two of them, and they're already cramped."

"When it comes to Vic, I don't think he minds being cramped with Stacy." I grabbed her phone and tossed it onto the bed before I snuggled with her again. My arms wrapped around her waist, and I held her close. "That means I need to rest as much as possible. You're on top for the rest of the night."

"That's fine with me. I like being on top."

"ONE...TWO..." Vic was squatting down with his hands hooked under the bottom of the couch.

"Do we need to count every single time? How about we just pick it up and move on?"

He glared at me. "I thought you'd like a good countdown, Rocketman?"

Now it was my turn to glare at him. "Let's just do this."

"Okay. One...two..."

"Jesus Christ, Vic. This thing is heavy."

"We would have been done by now if you just shut your mouth."

I rose to my feet and lifted up the couch, knowing the height change would force him to mimic me.

Vic picked up the couch and came level with me.

"Alright, was that so hard?"

"You tell me, Rocketman."

I ignored his taunts, and we carried the couch into the elevator and then into the U-Haul parked at the sidewalk. "Where's Stacy?"

"She's setting up dishes and stuff at the new house. Don't want her carrying anything heavy while she's got a bun in the oven."

"You wouldn't want her carrying anything heavy anyway."

"Yeah, probably not."

Charlotte emerged out from the doorway carrying one of the heavy wooden nightstands.

"What the hell are you doing?" I rushed to her and grabbed one side of the bedroom furniture, feeling how heavy just half of it was. "Why are you carrying this by yourself?"

"It's not that heavy, Neil. I got it."

I took it from her hands and carried it the rest of the way by myself.

Vic watched me, a knowing grin on his face.

I carried it into the truck then walked down the ramp once more. "Just stick to light boxes and stuff from now on."

"Come on, I'm stronger than that." She flexed her arm in her t-shirt, showing a slight bump of muscle that wasn't remotely impressive.

The last thing I wanted was for her to hurt herself, especially when I was leaving soon and couldn't take care of her. "Just do what I say." I couldn't keep my anger in check, couldn't keep my cool in front of my brother. I walked past her and headed back inside to grab the next item.

I could hear Vic's voice. "He means well. Don't be mad at him."

THEIR NEW PLACE was exactly where I imagined them living. It was a 3,500-square-foot house with hardwood floors, a southern porch outside, and a large backyard with a pool for the kids. Most of their furniture was perfect for the space, but since it was so much bigger than their apartment, they would need new additions.

Stacy had sandwiches on the kitchen island, turkey and cheese along with bags of chips for everyone.

Vic and I immediately grabbed a few sandwiches and stuffed our mouths as we stood there, both starving and irritable.

Stacy eyed us then looked at Charlotte. "Neil is just like his brother. Turns into an angry bear when he's hungry."

"He turns into an angry bear for other reasons too." Char gave me a glare before she picked up a box of towels and carried it down the hallway.

"What's that about?" Stacy asked, picking up a sandwich herself.

I was chewing, so Vic answered for me. "Charlotte picked up one of our heavy nightstands, and Neil lost his shit."

"She carried that by herself?" she asked incredulously. "Damn, she's pretty strong for not hitting the gym."

"Don't encourage her." I drank my iced tea, not impressed by her feat of strength. I already knew she was a strong woman for millions of reasons, but picking up something twice her weight and throwing out her back wasn't the best way to prove it. "So, I like your new place. It's really nice."

"Thanks," Vic said. "It was only on the market one day when we bought it. We hadn't even seen it in person when we made the offer."

"We just knew," Stacy said. "It's brand-new, and it's everything we wanted."

"I'm glad it worked out," I said. "I haven't taken an in-depth look, but I really like it. Great place for a couple of kids."

Stacy turned to Vic, trying to fight an affectionate grin from stretching over her face. "I know…"

Vic moved his arm around her waist then kissed her on the cheek.

Sometimes when I saw their affection, saw the way they visibly loved each other, it made me wish for a different life. It made me envision myself moving in to a place like this, Charlotte making lunch for everyone because she was the one who was pregnant. I'd never had those kinds of thoughts before, never had a fantasy like that. I used to think about dirty things, having sex in public places like in the back of my Range Rover. Now my fantasies were very different than they used to be. It seemed like something inside me had changed, just the way it did when Vic met Stacy, when Hyde met Jane.

Stacy watched me grip the counter and zone out. "Everything alright, Neil?"

I hadn't realized how much I'd spaced out until she mentioned it. "Yeah...just thinking about a few projects I have going on at work."

Vic stared at me like he didn't believe any of that. "Whatever you say, Neil."

———

"I don't appreciate you snapping at me like that in front of my family." She marched into the house first and was immediately bombarded by Torpedo. He rushed her and stood on his hind legs so he could get his tongue closer to her face.

She gave him a rubdown, but her anger was still directed at me.

"I didn't want you to get hurt."

"All you had to do was say that. But instead, you acted like a huge douche."

I followed her farther into the kitchen, watching her grab a beer from the fridge and twist off the cap. "Look, I've seen enough people get hurt in my line of work that I don't want it to happen to you."

"I'm not an astronaut, Neil."

"But you'd be surprised how little it takes to be crippled for six months." I snatched the beer out of her hand then backed her into the counter. My hands rested on either side of her as I boxed her in, forcing her face to be inches from mine.

When we got this close, she shut her mouth. Her eyes looked into mine, still angry but also kind. Her hands gripped the edge of the counter, and she took a deep breath when she felt our bodies together like this.

Just being this close to her reminded me of my feelings, reminded me how much I'd changed since we'd met. I used to be a playboy who broke beds as well as hearts. But when this little woman in her cutoff jeans walked into my life, I became a changed man. If only things were different...if only I could have both things. I'd chosen my fate, to be the first man in history to step foot on Mars, and that came with sacrifice.

Her breathing slowed as the silence trickled by. She became tenser the longer we stood like this, the longer we were close together and surrounded by our explosive heat. Her nipples hardened under her t-shirt, showing her arousal as well as her unease. We were wearing shorts and t-shirts because it'd been warm moving all that furniture, but now that the cold settled in, she started to shiver.

"It's my job to take care of you. My woman doesn't pick up anything heavy. I do that, alright?"

I only got a slight nod in return.

There was something I'd been meaning to give her, but I hadn't found the right moment. I didn't want to hand it over right before I left because it might make her sad afterward. I wanted to give it to her when we were still happy, before things turned sour. "There's something I want you to have." I dug my hand into my pocket and pulled out the white gold necklace I'd picked out at the jeweler. The pendant was an empty glass container, circular and closed off.

Her eyes went to the pendant, seeing the grains of sand inside. "What's that?"

"Sand from the moon."

Her eyes widened before she looked at me again. It was such a simple expression, but it conveyed every single thought inside her mind. It showed her emotions, showed her surprise. She released a deep breath as her eyes started to water.

"I got it from my favorite crater." I unclasped it then hooked it around her neck. It hung just above her breasts, so it was viewable with any article of clothing she wore. I watched it hang around her throat, knowing it looked exactly as I envisioned.

"I didn't know you were allowed to do that..."

"I'm not," I whispered. "But I did it anyway."

Her fingertips lightly touched the pendant as she looked me in the eye. A thin film of moisture was on the surface, reflecting the lights from the kitchen ceiling. It meant the world to her; that much was certain. "I don't know what to say..."

"You don't need to say anything." My fingers brushed against her cheek as they slid toward her hair. Her skin was so soft, like a rose petal in summer. My fingers slid into her hair, and I wrapped it around my fist, getting ahold of her like there was no gravity and she could drift away. I looked into her eyes and felt the pain radiate in my heart, felt the sadness from my upcoming departure. Any other man would make the same decision I had, but it didn't make it any easier. If I walked away from my colleagues now, I would be a traitor. I would lose all the respect I'd gained in my career. She wouldn't want me to stay anyway.

"I wish I could give you something to take with you..."

"You can."

"Well...what can you take?"

"A picture would be nice. PG, of course—since I won't have much privacy."

She smiled. "Alright, I'll find something."

SHE WAS ASLEEP BESIDE ME, on her side facing me with the necklace around her throat. Her hair was pulled back behind her on the pillow, and her arm rested on my waist as she breathed deeply, lost in sleep.

I wasn't tired despite moving all of Vic's furniture, so I observed all the subtle movements she made while she slept. I watched the way her lips would part then close again, studied the way her body looked so rested as she was deep in sleep.

It was a moment I wanted to treasure forever, a peaceful memory to lull me to sleep on the long journey to the far reaches of our solar system. In that kind of environment, it was hard to find a state of relaxation, physically or mentally. But all I had to do was think about this...and that would be enough.

I grabbed my phone from the nightstand, turned off the flash, and snapped a picture of her.

It was perfect.

HYDE WALKED BESIDE ME, his hands still dirty from working under the shuttle all day. "You think it's time?" We headed down the hallway to one of the conference rooms, the place where we met to discuss highly classified information that we didn't want the wrong person to hear.

"I think so." NASA had kept this mission a secret as long as possible because they didn't want to announce the voyage to the world if there was any chance we couldn't pull it off. But all of our engines were ready, our modules planned out, and the crew had passed all their exams.

It was really happening.

Hyde sighed beside. "Would you judge me if I said I was a little afraid?"

"No. Not at all."

"Good...because I'm a little fucking afraid."

I wanted to tell him he could back out, but that was a lie. It was too late to go back on our commitment. So, I fed his ego instead. "Whether we live or die, we'll be remembered for the rest of human history. Children will learn our names in school. We'll be the ones who charted the discoveries that will be made after we're gone. It's terrifying, but it's such an honor. You're lucky to be here, Hyde. I'm lucky to be here too."

The pep talk seemed to calm him because he nodded. "You're right, Neil. Thanks."

We walked into the conference room with the director and a few other members of the NASA team. The other four astronauts on the mission were there, two men and two women.

They all had different disciplines, so we could study as much as possible. Hyde and I were the only two crew members with the same background. If one of us died, there would always be another pilot to get us back home.

"Alright." Director Carmichael started the meeting. "We're going to have a press conference tomorrow morning and make our announcement to the American people and the world. This is officially happening. The launch takes place in exactly thirty days."

The last year had gone by so quickly, and I knew that was because of Charlotte. If she weren't in my life, time would have moved at a snail's pace. The launch date couldn't get there soon enough. But now, everything had changed. I was excited for this mission...but I was also filled with regret. It was the strangest feeling.

Hyde turned to me. "Man, my mom is gonna be pissed."

I didn't want to face my own family. Vic would be livid with me...and may not forgive me for what I was about to do.

20

NEIL

THE MOMENT I'D BEEN DREADING HAD FINALLY ARRIVED, AND I didn't have time to drag my feet and procrastinate anymore. Tomorrow morning, the entire world would know about the mission, and as the commander, my name would be mentioned first. It was a terrible way for my family to find out.

It had to come from me beforehand.

I considered telling Charlotte in private first, but then I would have to have the same conversation twice, and instead of breaking her heart first and moving on to the next person, I thought it would be best to tell everyone at once... in one shot.

I already knew how it would go. Charlotte would be sad internally but supportive on the outside. But she already knew what was coming even though she didn't have the details. Vic and Stacy would be totally blindsided, especially since I did the first of my two launches to the moon not quite a year ago. There was usually more time in between launches, but things had been different for me. This may be my final launch ever...even if I survived.

"Is there something bothering you?" Charlotte asked from the passenger seat.

I drove through the darkness to Vic's house, the streets wet from the rain that had fallen earlier. I was in a black sweater and a long-sleeved shirt. Charlotte was in a sweater dress with black leggings and boots. "I'm just stressed."

"About?" Her fingers absentmindedly played with her necklace as she looked out the window.

I wasn't going to tell her the truth on the drive, when I couldn't see her face because I was watching the slick roads. "You'll see when we get there."

I pulled into the driveway five minutes later, seeing the lights through the windows under the shady oak trees. Stacy was moving around in the kitchen, getting dinner ready because she expected us any moment.

Vic was on the couch, his feet up on the coffee table as he watched TV. Having Stacy at home full time was his dream. Now he had a woman to wait on him hand and foot while she had his children. He got to keep his exciting career and had someone waiting for him at home.

We helped ourselves inside. "Something smells good." Charlotte looked around, examining the round mirror on the wall and the new accessories Stacy had picked out. In just a few short weeks, Stacy had decorated the place and turned it into a home. "The place looks nice."

"Thanks, honey." Stacy greeted her with a hug then turned back to the kitchen. "Can you help me set the table?"

"Sure." Charlotte picked up a dish and started helping with dinner.

I moved to the other couch and looked at my brother. "How was work?"

"You know, bullshit like always."

"You call it bullshit, but you love it."

He shrugged. "I like yelling at people. It's fun."

I turned to the TV, seeing the game that was on the screen. "Got any money on this?"

"No." He turned to me. "Want to make it interesting?" He held his beer on his lap, his shoes off because he was so comfortable.

"A hundred bucks?"

"You're on."

Stacy called from the kitchen. "Dinner is ready. Neil, you want a beer or something else?"

"I'll have whatever you're having." I walked to the dining table and saw the mashed potatoes, green beans, and the chicken Marsala in a clear dish in the center.

Stacy grabbed a bottle of white wine and poured two glasses. "I'm having water. But Charlotte likes this bottle of wine, so you can have what she's having."

"Works for me." We took a seat by the window, and Stacy had to adjust her chair many times to accommodate her stomach.

"Oh my god, I'm so fat." She grabbed her water and took a big drink. "I should have done a surrogate."

Vic placed his hand on her thigh and gave her a gentle pat. "You aren't fat."

She rolled her eyes.

"And if you are, I like it." He grabbed the potatoes and served them onto his plate before he handed the dish to me.

Stacy had a small smile on her lips, like that meant the world to her.

Charlotte couldn't wait until all the food was served. She sampled whatever was on her plate as she waited for the next dish. "Ooh...these potatoes are good."

I served her a piece of chicken along with myself before we set everything back down on the table.

"What's new with you guys?" I asked, trying to keep the conversation light before I ruined everyone's night.

"The doctor says the baby is healthy," Vic said. "That's the only thing we care about anymore."

"Do you still not want to know if it's a boy or a girl?" Charlotte asked.

"No," Stacy answered after she chewed her bite. "We still want it to be a surprise."

We talked about that for a while before we switched the conversation to the weather. It'd been a rainy season in Texas, which was unusual. But we hadn't had any extreme storms. Hopefully, it stayed that way.

Stacy looked at the necklace hanging from Charlotte's throat. "What's that? It looks like dirt."

The texture of the sand on the moon was like fine powder. Whenever my boots sank into the material, I could feel how fluffy it was. Maybe because the force of gravity was less, the dirt wasn't so tight against the surface of the planet. It was also a different color from anything I'd seen on Earth, probably because it felt the radiation from the sun differently. Colors were washed out and bland.

Charlotte glanced at me, smiling slightly before she answered Stacy. "Neil gave it to me. It's sand from the moon."

Both Stacy and Vic both turned their gazes to me, understanding the significance of the gesture. I had no idea if Vic told Stacy how I felt about Charlotte, but I suspected he hadn't because he knew his wife couldn't keep a secret from Charlotte.

Vic kept giving me a look of accusation. "So, you got it last time you were up there?"

"Yeah," I said with a nod.

"That's sweet..." Stacy looked at the necklace again. "Are you allowed to do that? Did you need to submit it to NASA first?"

"No. I kept it in my pocket and hid it in my backpack until we returned to Earth." Even if I got caught, NASA wouldn't have prosecuted me. Just a slap on the wrist would have been enough. I was their best astronaut, and they couldn't afford to lose me or put the issue in writing. So, it was worth the risk for me to take it.

Charlotte played with the pendant before she started to eat again.

It was the perfect segue into the big news I needed to share, but I still didn't want to do it. It would change my relationship with Vic, make it more strained than it already was. Stacy would worry about me, and of course, Charlotte would have to accept the fact that I was leaving soon. It would spoil the evening.

But I had to do it.

I set down my utensils. "I have an announcement to make..."

"Oh no," Vic said. "Anytime Neil says that, it's not good. Going back to the moon already?"

"There's no way," Stacy said. "You would launch three times in the span of eighteen months. That's not right. It's unprecedented."

They were right on the moon—with the exception of the destination.

Charlotte stayed quiet and started to push her food around.

"I am launching again. Thirty days from now." I would have to climb into that rocket and explode with more fuel than ever before. I would travel farther than any living human, take on the most dangerous mission NASA had ever tried to accomplish.

Vic immediately looked down at his food, visibly pissed that I was departing once more. He shook his head slightly then cut into his chicken, continuing to eat because he didn't know what else to do. He kept his thoughts to himself because he knew he was about to explode.

Stacy was disappointed too. She didn't bother to hide it. "How long will you be gone this time?"

Before I could answer, Charlotte spoke. "No one is more upset about Neil's departure than I am. I wish he could stay here forever, or at least, take missions less frequently. I'll miss him every day while he's gone. But Neil is doing something incredible with his life, and we should all be supportive—and more importantly, proud."

Vic stopped eating, but he kept staring at his food.

It meant a lot to me that she said that, even though it would fall on deaf ears.

Charlotte kept staring at Vic. "Come on, Vic. Your brother is an extraordinary man. He's one in a million. You should be so proud right now."

"I am proud," he said bitterly. "I've always looked up to him. I feel like the coolest person ever when I tell people Neil Crimson is my brother. But no amount of pride can fill the void of his absence, or make me sleep at night and stop worrying about him every time he's gone. Don't tell me how to feel, Charlotte. Just don't."

Stacy turned to him. "Vic…"

"Charlotte knows I love her. But this is my brother we're talking about." He still wouldn't look me in the eye. "If he dies…"

"If I die, just know I wouldn't change anything if I knew that was my last moment alive." It was no different from the way a parent felt about their child. If they had to give up their life to save their son or daughter, they would do it in a heartbeat.

Vic finally raised his head and looked at me, his gaze cold.

Stacy rested her hand on his to calm him down.

"There's something else I need to tell you…and you aren't going to like it." I started to miss the fascination people had with my profession, all the questions they would ask because they were mesmerized about the things I'd seen.

My family didn't feel that way at all. They hated everything about my position as an astronaut.

"Let me guess," Vic said. "You'll be there for a year."

Stacy squeezed his hand to shut him up.

"Vic," Charlotte said gently. "Let Neil talk..." She was the only person on my side, the only person who understood she could feel sad about my absence but be supportive anyway. She was the only person who made this easier for me.

"Tomorrow morning, NASA is going to make an announcement to the world about the mission," I said. "It's the first time we've ever made this kind of attempt, but we've been planning it for years. I'm not going to lie, it'll be dangerous. Things will happen that we never would have anticipated. I'll be the commander of the mission with five other astronauts. Hyde is coming with me, so there will be two pilots."

Vic was still, watching me with wide-open eyes.

Stacy looked like she'd stopped breathing.

Vic finally spoke. "What does that mean, Neil? Where are you going?"

It sounded like a plotline from a science fiction movie, but it was all real. We'd progressed with our technology, but we hadn't told the world about our discoveries. We'd surpassed Russian technology a million times over, and now they would know they were inferior to our scientists. "Mars."

Charlotte took an audible breath that sounded like a gasp.

Stacy let go of Vic's hand so she could cover her mouth. "Oh my god."

Vic was in such a state of shock that he didn't move at all. He stared at me in silence until his body leaned back and collapsed against the chair. His hand went to his mouth, and he dragged it down his jaw. As if he couldn't bear to look at me, he turned away and stared at the floor. Then he got up and walked away from the table, as if he couldn't be around me a second longer.

Stacy didn't go after him.

Charlotte was in shock like everyone else. She stared at the surface of the table, not blinking because she processed everything I said with obvious pain.

I hadn't even told him the specifics of the mission, like our objective or the duration. They seemed to need time to process what I'd already said, so I stayed quiet. Their reaction was even worse than what I expected. I hadn't told my mother yet, and I knew that conversation would cause many tears.

I stared at my food because I didn't know what else to do. I didn't know how to cushion this blow, what to say to make this better. They were all scared for my well-being, and now they were probably truly afraid I would never come back.

21

CHARLOTTE

Neil's announcement was a shock to all of us.

People talked about going to Mars someday, but I assumed a mission like that would take place beyond our lifetime. Now the man I loved would be the commander of a mission that would travel past the moon...farther than any living human had gone before.

I was terrified.

Even if Neil and I would end our relationship the moment he left Earth, I would still love him for the rest of my life. If he didn't return, it would haunt me forever. For a split second, I almost gave in to the hysteria and asked him not to leave.

But it wouldn't make a difference.

Vic was sitting on the couch with his elbows on his knees. His palms were pressed together, resting against his lips. The TV was still on, but the sound was on mute. He stared at the low-burning flames in the fireplace, wrestling with his anger.

Stacy moved to the spot beside him and rubbed his back. "Vic…"

He ignored her.

Neil moved to the other couch and took a seat.

I didn't know what to do. Tears burned on the surface of my eyes, but I refused to let them fall. It would just make it a million times harder for him. Giving in to the pain wouldn't make anything better, it would only make it worse.

"Vic." Neil's deep voice came out quiet, tentative.

Vic ignored him.

Neil stared at the table.

I moved into the living room and sank into the armchair across from Neil. My body felt a million pounds heavier because of the stress that had settled on my shoulders. I knew I had to move on with my life when Neil left, but now I would still worry about him constantly.

Stacy continued to rub her husband's back. "I think he's just surprised…as we all are."

"I understand it's a lot to take in," Neil said. "I've known about this mission a long time, and I'm still surprised."

Vic slowly rubbed his palms together.

"How long will you be gone?" I asked, afraid to hear the answer.

Neil sighed, like he didn't want to tell his family the truth.

"The exact duration is uncertain, but probably around three years."

Oh my god.

Vic threw his arms down as he clenched his jaw. "You've got to be fucking kidding me. If you survive and make it back, my kid is gonna be three. I'll probably have a newborn too. And you're going to miss all of that?"

Neil looked away, swallowing the pain like a pill too big for his throat.

Three years was so long.

"Why the fuck do you need to be on Mars that long?" Vic snapped. "What's so important about a goddamn planet millions of miles away?"

"The time spent on Mars will be relatively short," Neil said calmly. "It's the journey that takes the longest. Based on the speed of our new spacecraft, it'll take nine months to get there. Another nine to return. The planets have to line up perfectly to create the shortest distance for us to travel. So we need to stay on Mars until the time is right because we can only carry so much fuel."

Vic dragged his hands down his face. "So, you're going to live on Mars for a year?"

Neil nodded.

"And do what?" he snapped. "What's so fucking interesting about red sand?"

Stacy squeezed his forearm. "Vic, calm down."

He pushed her arm off.

Now I understood why Neil wanted to break off our relationship. He would be gone for so long, there was no chance we could have a relationship. In three years, I might be married to someone else. We wouldn't pick up where we left off...not when that much time had passed. And he might not even survive.

"How stupid are you?" Vic snapped. "You're going to get yourself killed."

Like the brave man he was, Neil stayed calm. "That's always a possibility, but we've done everything we can to make sure that doesn't happen. We've never lost an astronaut in space before, and we aren't going to start now."

Vic shook his head, his jaw so tight. "If you die, my kid is never going to know his uncle."

"But he'll know my legacy," Neil responded.

Vic's clenched both hands into fists. "Fuck you, Neil."

I was upset too, but I didn't think Vic should talk to Neil like that. "Vic, if anyone can come back alive, it's your brother."

"Charlotte, not now," he hissed. "This is between family, alright?"

That stung pretty bad.

"Vic," Stacy hissed. "Calm down. Charlotte is a part of this family, and you know it."

Vic didn't apologize.

Neil looked at me, giving me sympathy when he was the one that deserved all the pity. "If it makes you feel better, this will probably be the last mission I'll ever do."

"Because you're going to die?" Vic asked coldly.

"No." Neil turned back to him. "Being in space that long will take a physical toll on my body. NASA will probably decommission me for space flight. I'll probably spend the rest of my career as an instructor for future astronauts and an engineer on their rockets and software."

It was the only thing that calmed Vic down. "I'll make a deal with you. Promise me this is your final trip, and I'll be supportive of this."

"Vic, don't put him in a position like that," Stacy said.

"I promise." Neil blurted out the answer without thinking about it.

Vic raised an eyebrow.

"I don't want to put you guys through this again," Neil said quietly. "And after being in space that long, I probably won't be eager to go back. And I won't be interested in the moon or the space station because that will be anticlimactic. This is what I've been training for my whole life. I'll lead the expedition to Mars, a monumental event I'll always be remembered for. Once I accomplish my greatest dream, it'll be time to move on to something else, prepare the next generation for space exploration. I can live with that."

Vic kept staring at his brother, like he was shocked by what he'd just heard. "I know you're a man of your word."

Neil nodded. "We have a deal?"

Vic would never be happy about this mission, but at least he had something to look forward to. His brother would be gone for three years, but if he survived, he would be on Earth for the rest of his life. "Yeah...we have a deal."

WE SAID nothing on the drive home.

We said nothing when we took off our clothes.

And we said nothing as we lay together under the sheets, Torpedo at the foot of the bed.

We still had a month together before he left this planet, but now that remaining time together had been poisoned by the knowledge of his departure. Now I really never would be able to live in the moment because I knew what was about to come.

I was so speechless, I couldn't talk. Now was the time to tell Neil how I felt, to ask all my questions in privacy. But I didn't feel like talking. I didn't feel like fucking. I didn't feel like doing anything.

Neil turned on his side and faced me, his eyes guarded because he didn't know what I was thinking. He stared at me, the sheets around his waist so his hard chest was revealed. He was totally naked, not because he expected sex, but because that was how we usually slept. "Are you okay?"

I nodded.

"You don't seem okay."

"Just a lot to take in..."

"Hyde will be with me. The rest of the crew are all experienced as well. We have some of the brightest minds in the world working on this project. It's not just the six of us on that ship. It's also everyone in the control center, all the scientists and engineers who are brilliant enough to even make this mission happen. Even when I'm millions of miles away in the deepest reaches of space, I'm never alone."

"I know...but I'll worry anyway."

"Please don't waste your time worrying about me."

That was impossible. Even if I somehow fell in love with someone else, I would always watch the news and ask Vic for updates. I wanted Neil to come back alive and well. That would make it easier for me to move on...to know he was safe. "I'll always worry about you, Neil. Even twenty years from now, I'll always hope you're well."

His hand moved to my stomach, and he gently stroked my skin. "You seem to be taking it better than Vic."

"I understand how important it is to you. Of course, I wish you were staying. Of course, I wish you were just an engineer who had a day job like everyone else. But I'm also proud of you for committing your life to something so amazing."

His eyes softened.

"I'm surprised you agreed to give it up."

"I have realistic expectations for this mission. It's going to be difficult and stressful. It'll take a toll on my mind and an even more adverse effect on my body. I'm still a young man by all accounts, but humans can only handle so much. Even if the flight surgeon clears me for another mission, I think it'll be time to step aside. I've made a lot of contributions to this profession, and you always want to go out on a high note. Great football players retire after winning a Super Bowl. Same idea."

"Too bad you didn't feel that way after your last mission..."

"A trip to the moon is child's play compared to this. I'll be one of the first humans to reach Mars, and I'll be remembered forever. That's a big accomplishment—and the best way to go out. I'll still be invigorated by my work with NASA and excited about training future astronauts and their work in space."

"For such an ambitious guy, that seems anticlimactic."

He shrugged. "I accomplished everything I ever wanted at a very early age. When you try to chase down the same thing over and over, it turns bland. Every time I go to the moon, I'm excited to be there, but it's never as good as my first visit. Just how it is."

"And you think you'll never want to go to Mars again?"

He considered my question. "If Mars were closer, that would be a different story. But it's so far away, such a long trek, that it won't be as appealing as a second time. I have to say...I thought you would be in agreement with my family. I thought you would be excited that I've decided to stay after this mission."

I'd be more excited if he weren't going on this mission at all. "I am. I'm just surprised you caved so quickly."

"I didn't cave. I suspected I wouldn't launch again anyway."

"And what if NASA asks you to?"

"I could always say my health can't handle it."

"But would you lie?"

He shrugged. "Even if I come back perfectly healthy, a mission like this is so stressful on the body. Maybe I could tolerate it once, but I doubt I could tolerate it twice. This is my dream and I'm willing to sacrifice anything to achieve it, but not if it means significant long-term damage to my body. Not worth it."

At least he had the logic to think this through.

He turned quiet, staring at me in the dark.

"Will I ever be able to talk to you? Send you a message?" Our relationship would be over, but it would be nice to see him as a friend, to give him some comfort while he was far away in the unknown.

"Yeah...you can send the videos to NASA, and they'll upload it to me."

"Will you be able to send videos back?"

He nodded. "Yeah...I can do that." His hand glided to my side, and he gripped my hip. "And I'll take that picture with me."

"I still haven't picked one out yet."

"Well, if you have several, I'll take them all."

"What?" she asked. "You're going to have a collage in your bunk?"

"No. I'll change out the picture every few months. I have pictures of Vic and Stacy too. Maybe I'll get a picture of their new baby before I go."

It was sweet that he didn't care about putting those pictures up in his personal area, even if other people saw them and thought he was weak. He was a macho man, but he definitely had a soft side he wasn't afraid to show. "I'm sure you will."

Neil turned quiet and stared at me, his eyes soft and filled with a hint of sadness. "I know this doesn't make a difference. I probably shouldn't say it. But a part of me wishes I didn't have to go..."

My heart thudded as I replayed that confession over and

over again in my mind. His meaning wasn't clear, and I didn't want to jump to conclusions. "What does that mean?"

"It means...I wish I could stay here with you."

"Is that even an option?"

He shook his head. "Even if I wanted to back out, I couldn't. There's not enough time to replace me."

"So, it would be illegal or something?"

"No. Technically, I can do whatever I want. But it would be sleazy to do that to my colleagues. It would push back the mission, which would be an embarrassment to NASA. I represent so much to the American people. Everything I do affects everything else. So, no...I wouldn't do that unless a family member were sick or something."

So even if he wanted to be with me, he couldn't stay. It would erase all the good things he had done in his career. It would make him look like a traitor.

"I just want you to know it is hard to leave...hard to leave all of you."

22

CHARLOTTE

"How are you holding up?" Stacy carried the dish of pasta to the table, her stomach so big, she could barely do anything anymore. It was hard for her to sit at the table because her belly was in the way.

"I think I should be asking you that." I grabbed the tongs and placed the pasta on the table.

She rubbed her stomach and sighed. "I've loved being pregnant...but I love not being pregnant more. Nine months is too long. They need to cut it down to four months or something."

"I don't think we have a say in that."

"But scientists do. Maybe they can speed up the process."

"At least you got lots of compliments while you've been pregnant. That you're glowing and stuff."

She rolled her eyes. "I'm not going to miss strangers touching my belly while I'm shopping at the grocery store.

And I feel so fat and ugly that I don't even want to have sex with Vic anymore."

"Stacy, Vic thinks you're so sexy."

She rolled her eyes again, this time more dramatically. "He just says that because he has to."

"I really don't think so. That's not what Neil says."

"What does Neil say?" She scooped the pasta onto her plate and started to eat.

"That Vic thinks it's sexy that it's obvious he knocked you up. It's like a pride thing, I guess."

She rolled her eyes a third time, but this time, there was a smile on her lips. "Back to you. Neil is leaving in two weeks, and you're—" Her hand reached for her stomach, and she sucked in a deep breath like she'd been struck with a white-hot bolt of pain.

"Stacy?"

"I think it was just the pasta. But—" She tightened again. "Oh my god..."

"What?" I was already on my feet, jumping to conclusions before she even had to tell me.

"My water just broke."

When I came to her side of the table, I saw the pool of liquid on the floor and the chair. It was still dripping over the edge. "I'll get your bag and put you in the car. I'll call Vic on the way."

"No, don't call him."

I grabbed the big bag from the closet and snatched my car keys from the counter. "What do you mean, don't call him?"

"He's in court until five because he has a big case. Just leave him alone."

"Stacy, you're having his baby. I'm going to call him." I grabbed her by the arm and helped her up.

"It's three o'clock. I can make it to five, alright? Just don't call him."

I helped her out to the truck in the driveway. "Stacy, if you have this baby and I don't call him—"

"Don't. Call. Him."

I GOT her to the hospital then into the private room. The nurse was getting her prepared, so I stepped out into the hallway. I texted Neil first. *Stacy is having the baby. Head over after work.*

After work? I'm leaving now. I'll pick up on my mom and meet you at the hospital. How's Vic?

Haven't told him yet.

And you told me first? Baby, call him.

Stacy doesn't want me to. He's in court.

Char, call him or I will. He doesn't give a shit about this case. He cares about his wife and his kid. Do it now.

I knew he was right, so I called. It rang and went to voice mail. He'd probably ignored my call because he assumed it wasn't important, so I texted him instead. *Stacy just went into labor. We're at the hospital.*

Vic called me back immediately. "When did she go into labor?"

"Her water broke about forty-five minutes ago."

"Then why am I hearing about this forty-five minutes later?" he spat.

"She didn't want me to bother you in the middle of your case."

"I don't give a fuck about this case. I'm sitting in the court-room now, looking the judge in the eye, and I don't give a shit. I'm leaving now." He hung up.

Damn...I didn't want to be up against him in a court of law.

———

NEIL and I sat in the waiting room with his mother.

"Excited to be a grandmother?" Neil asked her, sitting beside her while she watched the TV.

"Very. I know they're having two, so hopefully I'll have a grandson and a granddaughter."

"If they look anything like Stacy, they'll be cute," Neil said.

"You and your brother are so handsome," his mother said. "If they have a son who looks like Vic, he'll be adorable." She patted his hand gently.

I didn't know his mother very well, but she was sweet.

"I wish you would have some kids, Neil. You would be a wonderful father."

Neil looked at the TV, his eyes falling in sadness. "Yeah... maybe someday."

His mother turned to me. "What's new with you, Char?"

"Nothing big," I said. "I moved to a new hospital, so that's been nice."

"Oh, why did you move?"

I lied. "Better pay. I got a nice raise."

"Oh, that's wonderful," she said. "Make as much as you can. When you have your own family, you'll need it."

Like that was ever going to happen...

Neil changed the subject to protect me. "What's new with you?"

"Just taking Ambien so I can sleep at night...since my son is going to Mars." She wouldn't look at him.

Now I wanted to change the subject to help him out, but thankfully, the nurse came out. "We've got a healthy baby. Stacy is ready for visitors, so you're welcome to take a peek."

"OH MY GOD, HE'S BEAUTIFUL." I held little Victor in my arms and looked at his stunning brown eyes, identical to his father's. "He looks just like you, Vic."

"I know," Vic said proudly. "My little man."

"I'll have to chase all the girls away," Stacy said. "That should be fun..."

I handed him to Neil. "Ready?"

"Absolutely." Neil took him like a pro, like it wasn't the first time he'd held a baby. He looked into his nephew's face. "Definitely gonna be a ladies' man." He gently rocked him back and forth before he handed little Victor to his mother.

She beamed in joy. "My grandson..."

I smiled as I watched her hold her grandson, imagining myself doing the same in the future. I hoped to be surrounded by my children and my grandchildren one day, to make my own family that would comfort me in my final days. I knew having a child the natural way would be impossible, that he would never have my husband's eyes, but he would still be my son all the same.

I had an epiphany in that moment, that Neil would never be that man. I may love him deeply, but he would never give me the future I wanted. Seeing my best friend so happy with her husband and newborn son made me realize it was time to move on with my life. I needed to find a man who wanted what I wanted, who wanted to have a family with me even if I couldn't give birth to his children.

I loved Neil...but he wasn't the man I should love.

Maybe Kyle was right...I made the wrong choice.

"YOU HAVE A SUPER CUTE NEPHEW." I walked in the door, and Torpedo immediately rushed me to give me a kiss.

"I know." Neil walked in behind me, handsome and strong in his cotton shirt. He peeled off his brown jacket and hung it on the rack. "He really is. Vic and Stacy did a good job. I'm sad that I won't see him grow up for the first three years."

"You'll see him when you get back..." I rubbed Torpedo behind the ears before I stepped away.

"Yeah..."

I grabbed Torpedo's bowl then set it on the counter so I could add the dog food. "You still never want to have kids?"

He shrugged. "Probably not."

"Even if you never go back into space?" I added the food then returned the bowl to the ground so he could eat.

"I'll probably still move around to different facilities. I'll be in Florida working on stuff, and there's another lab in Pasadena they might send me to. I'll never be in one spot too long, so it wouldn't be fair to them."

It broke my heart all over again. Even if he stayed on Earth, he would still never be around. There really was no hope for us ever. If I didn't want children so much, I might not care... but I wanted a family more than anything in the world. The way Neil felt about space was the way I felt about kids.

I kneeled down and rubbed Torpedo again, comforting myself more than him.

Neil leaned against the counter and watched me.

I ignored his look as long as I could, not wanting him to know what was bothering me. I eventually rose to my feet and washed my hands in the kitchen sink. "Want to watch a movie?"

"It's pretty late. I have work in the morning."

I wouldn't be able to get any sleep tonight. Probably not for the foreseeable future either. In two weeks, Neil would blast off on a grand mission.

Neil kept watching me. "Everything okay?"

"Yeah, I'm fine." I grabbed a glass and filled it with water from the fridge. When it was full, I took a long drink, mostly to cover my reaction.

"Char."

I forced myself to turn around, to keep up the illusion everything was fine.

Neil saw right through it. "We tell each other everything. Don't hold out on me now."

"It's nothing…"

He crossed his arms over his chest, refusing to move until the conversation happened.

I set the glass down. "Being around Vic and Stacy just reminds me of what I want. I want to get married and have a family. I know I'm young and I still have plenty of time, but when Cameron and I started trying, I was ready. Now I have to start all over…and I don't want to. That should be me right now."

Neil didn't blink, keeping his emotions hidden under the surface. "It'll happen when it's meant to happen."

How could it ever happen if I wasn't with the right guy? My husband left me when I couldn't give him kids, even though I wanted them more than he ever did. And now I was dating a guy about to launch into space for three years who never wanted kids. What the hell was wrong with me? I had a nice man who loved me, who would give me everything I wanted, and I didn't appreciate him when I should. Maybe I was in love with Neil in a way I never would be with Kyle… but in the end, it didn't matter.

Neil crossed the space between us then slid his fingers into my hair. "I promise, it'll happen when it's meant to happen. Don't let Stacy and Vic make you feel like a failure. One day, that's going to be you. Maybe you'll have kids in a different way, but those kids will be yours...and you'll be happy."

23

NEIL

"I'm surprised you have time to get a drink." We were at the bar, sitting in our usual booth. "You've got a baby at home. I figured you'd want to be with him."

"Yeah, but you're leaving in a week. Victor will be screaming and crying long after you're gone."

"Does he cry a lot?" I asked with a laugh.

"Unless he's sucking on Stacy's tit."

I chuckled. "So, he's just like you."

He laughed then drank from his beer. "I'm gonna miss you, man. Every time you're gone, I can't wait for you to get home. I get a calendar and count down the days."

All the laughter died in my throat.

"Then when you're here, you aren't here long enough for us to get close again. But this is your last mission... I keep telling myself that."

He made me feel like shit so easily. "We are close, Vic."

"Yeah, but we'd be so much closer if we saw each other all the time. Then when you aren't here, all I do is listen to Mom bitch about it. It'll be nice when you're back for good. Maybe you can settle down and have a normal life."

Charlotte really wanted to have a family, and judging by the way she got so emotional about Vic and Stacy, she wouldn't wait three years until I came back...especially when I still didn't want kids. She had her priorities, and I didn't fit into her five-year plan. After Victor was born, everything changed. She was more distant with me, like she was prepared for the breakup before it even happened.

It sucked.

"What are you going to do about Charlotte?"

I knew he would ask eventually. "What do you mean? I'm leaving. We have to break up."

"You aren't even going to tell her how you feel?"

"No." That would be cruel. If I told her I loved her before I left, she would never be able to move on. It was easier to assume there was no future instead of clinging to hope. Even if I returned and wanted to stay put, I still couldn't offer her anything she wanted. We were doomed...and I wouldn't waste her time the way Cameron did. "And you better not tell her."

He raised both hands in the air. "Come on, you know I'll take your secrets to the grave. I just wonder if you should... just in case you don't come back."

"If that happens, then I really don't want her to know. It'll just hurt her more."

He shrugged. "Maybe."

"You're finally getting what you want, Vic. I'll be gone, and she can move on."

"You think that's what I want?" he asked incredulously. "If I had it my way, the two of you would get married and pop out a few kids. That's what I would want. But since you're stubborn and refuse to give her that...even if you love her... then letting her go is the best thing you can do. I agree with your decision."

Without Charlotte, I felt so empty inside. It would be a long and painful departure into space...with only a couple of pictures to comfort me.

Vic continued to watch me. "It's not too late, Neil."

"It is too late. And even if it weren't...I have to do this. I'll regret it for the rest of my life if I don't."

"Then you'll regret losing Charlotte instead... You're damned if you go, and you're damned if you stay."

I PACKED up my things and put the important stuff into storage. I'd turned over my house to a property management team so they could rent it out to someone for the next three years. If I died during the mission, my will would instruct my lawyer how to divide my assets.

It was depressing, packing up my things like I may never return.

Charlotte helped herself inside, Torpedo with her on a leash. "Wow, this place looks bare."

"Yeah...don't want anyone to steal my stuff. I'm just leaving the big furniture. All my medals and uniforms are going to the storage facility." My family pictures would go into storage as well. If I passed away, my brother would get all of that stuff.

She joined me on the couch, her hand resting on my forearm. "You doing okay?"

I stared at my hands and didn't speak.

"This must be hard for you…"

"I've never left for such a long duration. Six months is my max. Three years…is a long time."

"Yeah…" She rubbed my arm.

"I have to go to Florida tomorrow. That's where we're launching."

"Oh…I didn't know that."

Because I didn't tell her. I wanted this break to be as clean as possible. I wanted to minimize the pain, make it as easy for her as possible. The less she knew, the better. I wanted to tell her how much I would miss her, that I would miss her even more than my own family. But I kept my mouth shut.

She rested her cheek against my shoulder and closed her eyes. "I'm gonna miss you so much…"

I turned my lips to her forehead and gave her a kiss. "I know…I'm gonna miss you too."

I'D LEAVE my Range Rover at the Houston center until I returned. They would change the battery and turn on the engine every month to keep it going. I wouldn't have to worry about someone else taking care of it or someone stealing it out of my driveway.

I woke up that next morning, dead tired because I didn't sleep. Charlotte and I didn't make love all night like I'd imagined we would. We were both too depressed. We didn't make small talk either, because all we could think about was the moment I had to leave.

Vic and Stacy weren't coming to the launch, not when they had Victor now. My mom wasn't coming either because it was just too hard. A part of me wanted Charlotte to be there, but I knew it was best if she stayed home.

I stood at the kitchen counter and watched the sun rise over the horizon. A cup of coffee was next to my hand, but I didn't drink it. It was a frozen February morning, and the excitement I normally felt for a launch was nonexistent.

I was dead inside.

Charlotte woke up thirty minutes later, and she came up behind me and wrapped her arms around my waist. Her cheek pressed against my back, and she breathed a painful sigh.

I didn't want to turn around and face her. I didn't want to see the heartbreak in her eyes. I was leaving for so long, and even if I returned alive, everything would be different. Charlotte would be a whole new person.

I would be a new person.

I turned around and faced her, my arms wrapping around her for comfort. Our foreheads came together, and we held each other in the kitchen. The silence was somber, making our heartbeats so loud.

Then she started to cry...like she couldn't take it anymore.

It was the first time I wanted to cry too.

My hand moved into her hair, and I kissed her tears away. I did everything I could to make her feel better, to mask the pain we both felt. I held her tighter, wanting to savor the affection during my long nights alone.

We stood together like that for nearly an hour, never wanting to break apart.

Then the doorbell rang.

It was my family coming to say goodbye.

I opened the door and didn't bother with a smile. I was depressed...and they were depressed. This wasn't a launch to the moon that would normally be filled with enthusiasm. To them, this was a death sentence.

They all came inside, baby Victor with them.

My brother handed him to me right away, letting me hold him before I had to leave. The car service company would be there any minute to pick up my things and take me to the center. Then they would put me on a plane so I could be in quarantine before launch. I held my nephew close, thinking about all the years I would miss. "Word of advice, little man. If you see a girl you like, don't pick on her. Just tell her." I handed him off to Stacy, who already had tears in her eyes.

The car pulled up to the front of the house.

Time was passing so strangely in that moment. It was going by so fast, but so slowly at the same time.

I said goodbye to my mother first. I held her for a long time, and when I pulled away, she was holding back her tears. She didn't say anything because she couldn't bring herself to speak. Instead, she blessed me, pressing her fingers into my body to make a cross.

I nodded. "Thanks, Mom."

She sniffled when I turned away.

I hugged Stacy next, letting her cry into my chest while she held her son. "Please be careful. We need you to come home…"

"I'll do my best." I kissed her cheek then moved to my brother next.

It was the first time I'd seen Vic cry…or at least, his form of a cry. His eyes were wet with emotion, enough to reflect the light from the ceiling. He stared at me, his jaw tight like he was trying to steady his quivering lip.

I moved into his chest and hugged him.

He hugged me back.

We stood that way together for a long time, both on the verge of breaking down into sobs.

"I love you, brother," he whispered into my ear.

"I love you too." I patted him on the back and turned away.

Charlotte was my last goodbye.

And the hardest.

I sighed as I looked at her, unsure what to say.

Tears fell down her cheeks because she had the weakest restraint out of everyone. She wore her heart on her sleeve, let her eyes go puffy and red from despair.

I reached into my back pocket and pulled out the collection of five pictures she gave me. "You'll always be with me." I held them up for her to see, not showing her the last one in the pile. "And I'll always be with you." I pressed my finger to the pendant around her neck.

She cried harder then moved into my chest to hug me. She gripped me tighter than she'd ever had, sobbing into my shoulder and convulsing with pain. She didn't care about the opinion of my family. She didn't care what anyone thought of us. Then she pulled back and kissed me, her lips wet with salty tears.

I cupped her cheek and kissed her back, my lips trembling with emotion.

When I pulled away, I knew I needed to walk out that door without looking back. If I stayed, I would break down too. I grabbed my bag from the floor and stepped back. "I love you all..." I turned and walked out the front door, managing to get into the back seat of the SUV before I lost my nerve.

The driver pulled away from the curb, and that's when it hit me.

I may never see Charlotte again.

And that's when the tears escaped.

24

CHARLOTTE

Are you sure you don't want to come over? Stacy texted me for the third time that night.

I'm okay.

I'm serious. Sleep over.

This was a special time in their lives, when they wanted to spend time with their new baby. I didn't want to get in the way of that with my heartbreak. *I'm fine, really. I've got Torpedo here.* Normally, I would have Kyle, but we stopped talking three months ago. Hadn't seen him since.

Vic is a wreck, and I know you must be worse.

I threw up that morning because the night was rough. I was used to him sleeping beside me every single night. Now the only thing left was his smell. I wouldn't wash the sheets for a long time to preserve his presence as long as possible. *Neil is doing something incredible. I'm happy for him.*

You can be devastated for yourself and happy for him at the same time.

I put my phone away and went back to the bed, hoping to sleep away my pain until it wasn't there anymore.

THE NEXT DAY, I threw up again.

I filled the toilet with my dinner, leftover pizza and hot wings.

I went to work as usual, mindlessly doing my job without caring like I usually did. On my lunch break, I ate alone in the corner. Neil hadn't texted me, and I didn't text him either. It was too hard for both of us, so it was easier just to let it be.

When I went home, I immediately changed into my pajamas and got into bed.

Torpedo whined at me with his leash in his mouth because he wanted to go for a walk.

"Not today, Torpedo." I rolled over and faced the other wall. The silence was deafening, so I turned on the TV just to have noise in the background. I lay there so still that I fell asleep, woke up at nine in the evening, and then went back to sleep. I didn't even have dinner.

THE NEXT MORNING, I was working in the lab when I had to throw up again.

It was the third morning in a row.

The first thing that popped into my head was pregnancy. Stacy went through this almost every day of her first trimester. She had a favorite stall at work she liked to puke in. But since that wasn't possible with me, I knew it was something else.

Maybe something more serious, like an infection I'd contracted in the lab. I handled biohazardous waste on a daily basis. It wasn't ludicrous to think I'd ingested something by mistake. There was a lot of deadly bacteria out there, stuff that could even cause cancer.

Oh shit, what if I had cancer?

On my lunch break, I made an appointment to see my primary care provider. Maybe he could run some tests and figure out what the problem was.

When I got off work, I went home to do my evening routine, but this time, I took Torpedo on a walk. If I didn't, he would pester me all night, which was fair…because I hadn't been a good mother.

Tomorrow, Neil's rocket was going to launch into the sky.

I wasn't sure if I was going to watch it.

How could I watch the man I loved leave this earth? Possibly forever?

After our walk, I lay in bed once more, expecting to drift in and out of sleep until I had to go back to work.

That was when Cameron called me.

"What the hell?" I squinted as I looked at his name on the screen. I answered, assuming it was important. "Uh…hi?"

"Hey, sorry for calling so late. I need to talk to you about something."

"Alright…everything okay?"

"Yeah, everything is fine. I'd just been thinking about what happened with us and what happened with Vivian and I. At first, I thought maybe I was the problem...since I can't seem to father a viable baby. I convinced myself that I was just being paranoid, that it was just a coincidence. Well, I went to a different facility to run some tests...and I'm the problem. Last time we went to the fertility doctor, she said you were unable to conceive...but now I think they got our paperwork mixed up."

Stunned, I just listened to him, my stomach tight with tension.

"So, there's nothing wrong with you, Char. You can have kids. I'm the one who can't..."

I was practically hyperventilating, so ecstatic I couldn't think straight. But I was also terrified, because I hadn't been on birth control in a year, and Neil and I...oh my god.

"Char?"

"Sorry, I have to go."

———

It was ten in the evening when I ran to the drugstore and picked up a pregnancy test.

Jesus Christ, I was about to take a pregnancy test.

I did my business then let the stick sit on the counter. Two minutes had to pass before the results were in. Two minutes was nothing, but in that instance, it felt like an eternity. I sat on the toilet with my fingers covering my bottom lip.

"Oh my god..."

A part of me didn't want to be pregnant because it wasn't supposed to happen this way. I wanted to be married, or at least be with a partner who also wanted kids. But Neil didn't want a family. He didn't even want a wife.

But another part of me hoped I was pregnant anyway... because this was my dream.

It was my dream to be a mom.

When two minutes passed, I looked at the results.

Pregnant.

"Oh my god...oh my god."

IT WAS MIDNIGHT, and Neil was launching first thing in the morning. In fact, it was one a.m. there. He was dead asleep, trying to get as much as rest as possible before he launched. I considered calling him and waking him, telling him this life-changing news.

But I also steadied myself.

Telling him now was the worst possible time. He was about to explode into the unknown, about to take a dangerous journey he may not survive. Dropping this bomb on him, that he was going to be a father, would be selfish.

Catastrophic.

So, I shouldn't tell him.

But if I didn't tell him now, when would I tell him?

When he came back in three years?

By then, I would be just a memory to him. He would be in a

new place. He might fall in love with one of the female astronauts. He would be in such a different headspace that having a kid would be the worst thing.

To have a kid with a woman he didn't even love.

He said he didn't want kids, said he wouldn't change his mind about it.

Did I want my child to have a father who didn't want him?

No. Probably not.

I could do this on my own. I owned a home, had a good job, and had a great dog. I didn't need a man.

But Stacy and Vic would know. They would assume it was Neil's. At some point, I'd have to tell them...unless I lied and said it belonged to someone else.

But who?

I WENT to Stacy's house the next morning.

It was so hard to sit there with my secret, to know I had spectacular news but couldn't tell anyone.

"You okay?" Stacy watched me with Victor in her arms. The rocket was on the TV, getting ready to start the countdown any moment.

"Yeah...I'm okay." I felt strange keeping this secret, not telling my best friend what I'd just found out. But the news wouldn't change what was about to happen. Even if Neil wanted to stay in light of this news, it would humiliate him in front of the entire world. Saying nothing was the only thing I could do. And I didn't want to make a bad situation worse.

Vic sat on the other couch, visibly stressed by the launch. "It's the biggest rocket they've ever created. A lot could go wrong..."

"Don't talk like that," Stacy said.

"Neil was part of the process and did the final checks himself," I said. "It'll be okay..."

Vic sighed, like he couldn't believe that.

We stopped making small talk, and minutes later, the countdown began.

One minute.

I'd been hoping to see Neil one last time, to see him entering the structure to board the rocket. All I saw were six people in white space suits from a distance. I assumed the man in front was Neil, but I couldn't be certain.

Thirty seconds.

Maybe I should have told Neil I loved him, just so he would know. But if he really paid attention, he would have figured it out on his own. I wouldn't let myself get hurt again unless he also made me joyously happy.

Ten seconds.

Vic moved to the couch between Stacy and me and held both our hands.

Five seconds.

Once that rocket was gone, it would be time for me to move

on. I wasn't sure what to do with Neil's baby, if I wanted to be honest about the father or keep it a secret, but regardless, our relationship was over. Once he was gone, everything was gone.

One second.

The rocket ignited, fire and smoke erupting around the bottom. We were states away, but I could feel the vibration under my feet. The enormous rocket left the surface of the Earth and slowly rose to the sky.

"We have lift-off."

The rocket took off, exploding into the sky, flying through the clear blue as it headed to the atmosphere. It would only take two minutes to reach the stratosphere, and the camera followed the rocket as long as it could.

It kept going…and going.

When the camera couldn't capture it anymore, the network cut to the reporters on the screen. "We'll give more updates once NASA notifies us about the progress of the mission, the world's first attempt to reach Mars."

I hadn't even realized I was crying until I felt the tears reach my lips.

Stacy was crying too.

Vic was the only one who stayed calm, but he seemed just as upset as both of us. "He made it…he made it."

Stacy sighed. "Let's just hope he makes it all the way home."

Made in the USA
Middletown, DE
20 March 2021

35889694R00177